A DOORSTEP MIRACLE

BY

RENEE SIMONE WELLS

New Generation Publishing

You hear about it all the time. A man is given a month to live. He has a tumour, developing rapidly like a high speed wind but survives, lives and departs from this life when his time is right. Children, born blind but with age, regain the ability to see. Miracles. But, the miracle that I am going to be writing about, is not one you would read on billboards or see when watching the evening news eating dinner with your family. No, this miracle, you could say (or as I like to call it) was 'A doorstep miracle'.

Initially, Dr Harvard physically fulfilled without any doubt, the Science-is-life high school teacher stereotype. He was a sociologist's most desirable example validating the theory of a self-fulfilling prophecy. But what I came to realise about Dr Harvard was such an opposition against what any person would perceive, beyond what imagination can provide. Because you see, the thing about life, is that it can surprise you, so that what you believe to be impossible is in actual fact a concealed reality, hidden temporarily under a façade, pretending that it doesn't exist; scared to subvert expectations. Sometimes all it takes is for someone to tell you that you can recover what you once lost, or what you thought you were incapable of discovering. And so, I decided that this winter, I would be the person to light a flame never once before lit and to challenge possibility with everything I knew, taking into consideration all consequences. And if you asked me "would you do this all over again?" I would answer with confidence "Absolutely."

1

The unexpected pleasure of meeting Dr Harvard

It was a frosty Monday morning and winter had never been so prevalent, the novelty of ear muffs, numb faces and the way that leaves crushing underneath your feet sounded like crunchy-nut Cornflakes engulfed me. Oh it was winter alright. It was my duty as a teacher and respected figure throughout Crenshaw Heights School, to advocate the wearing of hats, gloves, scarves and of course, I'd better not forget… ear muffs. However, what I later on had the delightful pleasure of experiencing was not at all what I expected. It all began in my year 12 English Literature class with a …

"Ms Dakota?" Jed Waters confidently bellowed at me from the very back of the room. Jed was the type of student who thought he knew everything about anything. A classmate's nightmare I can imagine. What's more, he was relentlessly arrogant and rude, or should I say considering my position, 'self-assured.' He showed extreme talented during out-loud reading and role-play, but then again, this was largely based on the disguise of an insecurity amounting to unimaginable proportions.

Yes Jed, what would you like to ask?" I said with an adolescent 'oh really?' sigh in my voice. He stared, eyes glowing with adrenaline, like the best thing you've ever heard was about to spill right from his mouth.

"Art thou rather annoyed with oneself for choosing to take up such a job that closes thy eyes with boredom?" He replied with a look of self-righteousness smothered all over his face. He now had the entire class giggling uncontrollably. Simply, I did not take this to offense. In fact, I couldn't decide what was more offensive, Jed's poor attempt to imitate Shakespeare or his surreptitious dig at my choice of job. I was prepared for teenage jokes, remarks made out of context and even for immaturity. But what I was not prepared for, more than anything, was for what I heard next.

"It's just that I'm speaking on behalf of Doctor Harvard. Ask anyone here and they'll defend me." Jed smirked, with his chest puffed out like he'd won the world war single-handedly, however, found it an obligatory action to seek approval from his army with a long gaze directed at each, individual student.

"Is that right? And who is this Dr Harvard? Does he work at the hospital across the road?" I asked, scanning my eyes across all faces in my classroom. I noticed each and every one appeared incredulous, as though I were supposed to know who this man was.

"Seriously, Ms, you haven't been introduced to Doctor Harvard? He's new. He's been here for like two weeks and his teaching methods are cool as hell." Jed replied, followed again by outrageous laughter from the class.

In that moment, it seemed that all professionalism was lost and faded behind the cloud of rage that shrouded my logic's eye. But I somehow managed to find it again, maintaining composure. *God*, I thought to myself. I need a God damn cigarette. I need a God damn cigarette, so I kept telling myself. I kept on replaying this sentence in my head on repeat, allowing it to devour my strength, and for what? A group of inconsiderate, rebellious, unhygienic and arrogant adolescent boys accompanied by moody, self-centred, menstruating bitches. They didn't care about what I had to say. I was not naïve to this. Incuriosity is a sin, and God knows these guys were sinners. I didn't want to hate my job and I didn't originally hate my job but it never used to be a job. It used to be my life, my passion, my purpose. But this was an irrelevant anecdote, which many sitting in that classroom would not even attempt to understand.

"Okay, Jed, I would really appreciate it if you used a more imaginative oxymoron but it's fantastic to know that you're enjoying lessons." I smiled calmly, secretly pleased with myself. I resumed with the lesson. My comment received a wave of laughter, just like the one that Jed managed to generate when I was the joke. Well, now he was the joke and I finally knew for once in my life how it felt to be noticed, given the chance to be popular and worshiped like a God. Goddess of the classroom was my name I had decided for that day. Anyway, after a while of silence, I was, as predicted, propositioned again.

"Ms I feel bad cus' he's been preachin' about how English is like I don't know, kind of lame? He says it's an excuse for sad people to claim they have achieved artistic excellence or whatever. Says it shouldn't even be considered an academic subject and that it has no meaning. I mean, d'you think he's right? I mean, he's a Dr and they're always right Ms." I was shocked. Every single student appeared as though they of trusted this opinion (if it had even been said). I couldn't believe it, I was actually angry for once, undermined and demeaned, humiliated in front of teenagers; a group of soon-to-be adults. Everything I believed in was negatively exploited, inaccurately represented and it angered me, more than it should have. But I had to remain calm for the sake of employment. I couldn't let them see me this way about a subject that for many of them was just a ticket to enjoy the nightlife at a University which, if they kept following the crowd, they would fail to receive an offer from. But it was more than that for me. Writing was my life and my belief and eventually, became, as a socially recognised and constructive use of my existence; a job. If I failed to defend it then who was I and what did I stand for?

"Is that so? And what does this Dr Harvard teach?" I asked, maintaining self-control and refusing to let these comments offend me.

"Science Ms, specialising in physics." Jed replied looking rather guilty and nervous himself, forcing me to question whether this was all just one big misunderstanding, as I'm sure it was. And by 'misunderstanding' I meant that this was a premeditated calculation of negativity, condensed in the form of an invisible bullet that would be, as intended by Jed Waters, invisibly shot right through the centre of my chest. But of course, I had to convince myself if the argument that people are misinterpreted all of the time and this was probably just another classic case of social twister. I was prepared to arrive at a logical and mature conclusion in no time at all.

"Ah, interesting." I smiled at Jed Waters and his army of stoned, lethargic students. How they thought they had ever gotten to me was a thought I found quite the height of hilarity.

It was the end of the lesson and I had dismissed everyone from their seats. I had to speak to this Doctor and find out whether or not this was true. I felt like a school girl again, taunted by the mean things girls said that would eat away at me until I truly felt like nothing. How silly it feels now to think that I thought I was going to end it all at that age… planning an escape, racking my brains for an explanation to justify my disappearance. 'Kids…eh?' My mother would say to all of her friends to try and rationalise my mistakes. 'Don't be silly I told myself, it's nothing, you're a woman now, just leave it for another juvenile mind to worry about.' And lord there were plenty of those sitting in that classroom. If this Doctor Harvard had really said this to my students, I was going to find out why.

Locking the door behind me, I started to walk towards the laboratories. I had always despised science as a young girl, purely because of the conditions, experiments and the fact that all of the answers had to be correct. This was a monstrous obstacle as, I myself, was not correct nor in any way could I have been considered a prime example of the model teenage conformist. Oh but when I wrote, oh when I write, there doesn't have to be any right answers. In fact, that's why I was utterly compelled to write. When you see a pen, a pencil, of course the initial thought would be that this object allows you to write. But when I saw this object sitting in front of me, all I saw, all I can ever see is possibility. It was the closest thing to magic that I had ever felt. It provoked a fire in me that can never be extinguished. And that burning, it supressed, lay dormant for a while but once fuelled, was indestructible. Oh but I am not fooled by this so called 'talent'. This so called 'gift'. Because to feel everything is both a blessing and a curse. But to always want to write what one feels, oh, it is the reliving that is a curse.

I could be my imperfect self, and it wouldn't matter. And tears did not have to fall anymore because they were substituted by words, channelling, even more effectively or, as this education system would refer to it as; academically, my pain. I was my best self when I was writing and it had always been this way. But walking down these corridors, I became immediately claustrophobic. Posters of photosynthesis, DNA structures and numbers presented in all their infinite excellence were what squashed me and all I believed in. I was a follower, a believer in a faith that was exiled by all who heard of its prophecy and it scared me so, we writers were always put on the endangered species list. I was suffocating. A child's fears, I read once always stay with a person, even when they grow old. I suppose you could say that ghosts really do exist.

I must have been expressing my fear out loud, for a sudden squeak of a shoe I heard behind me turned out to be a man, like one acting in the American sci-fi drama *'House'*. He was tall, thin and wearing a conventional professor's lab coat whilst fiddling with some sort of scientific device of which I was unfamiliar. He stared with blank, empty eyes the colour of a rainy day grey. His hair possessed the vitality and youth that all women desired. He wore glasses with harsh frames, bland in colour, a sort of non-descript green. He had an awkward demeanour yet stood with confidence, adamant he was correct in whatever it was that he was doing. He was and still is the most intriguing man I had ever set my eyes on. He was enigmatic, electric, and magnetic.

After staring for some time in absolute silence, he then spoke.

"L…Lost are we?" he stammered followed by a nervous laugh. I could not tell whether he had a speech impediment or whether he was simply just shy. I knew I was, I was more than shy. I hated to admit it but I was intimidated.

"Uh… yes, well, I mean no, ha-ha. I am looking for and wish to speak with Dr Harvard. Do you know where I could find him?" I smiled politely whilst analysing the object he held.

His eyes immediately widened. His pupils were almost, you could say, dilated. Something I had said did not settle well with this man.

"May I ask which department it is you work for?" He focused seriously now on my eyes, as though he would be able to tell if I were lying. He rose his chin and tipped his head backwards in anticipation.

"I work for the English department down on the third floor sir, may I ask why this is of interest to you?" I asked, scared at what his reaction may be, as, I could sense an atmospheric contempt.

It was as though a switch had been turned. His tone changed from neutral and fairly polite, to sharp and hostile as if I had annoyed him in some way by my response. This was then further established by his reply.

"Ah. I see. Dr Harvard does not wish to speak with you I'm afraid. He is extremely busy." He then turned abruptly, opened a laboratory door and slammed it with force. I was confused and really quite baffled at this inexplicable impoliteness. But I was not going to let this stop me in my search for Doctor Harvard. I needed to resolve this and to prove wrong the accusation that had come to my attention earlier this morning.

"Why is that?!" I shouted. There was no answer. All that remained was the echoing of my voice down those dreaded corridor walls. That voice I heard seemed in isolation, perpetual. I felt again, alone and confused in my position and I did not know whether it would be a wise decision to knock on the door which, had not moments ago been slammed in my face. Why, of course, of course it was a wise decision. It had never stopped me before. And so, I stood wracked with contemplation until courage tempted me with an encouraging push. I couldn't believe what I was doing, but I was at this door, the door that had banished me by a man who seemed to hate me without reason. It came somewhat ironic to me, how a man, interested in a subject with conditions being its central foundation that he had not justified this one with an answer.

A Doorstep Miracle

I demanded to know why Dr Harvard would not like to speak with me to discuss my concern. I needed this man to tell me where this famous Doctor Harvard was, or whether he was even real. There was no doubt in my mind that the classroom army would have gathered together and made this up simply for some form of entertainment, during my oh-so-boring lessons.

I pushed open the door with force. The man I had just met sat there staring at me in disgust. He said nothing, not a single word but I could read from his facial expressions that he disliked me very much. My persistence aggravated him. In his eyes I must have been a child, badgering their mother desperately for a toy which they neither truly wanted nor had the intention of playing with on the shelf in a shop.

"Why doesn't Doctor Harvard wish to speak with me? And where is he?" I was frantic. I didn't know why, but I was becoming nervous. My palms were sweating, my face burning up and my exterior body tensing in a state of paralysis.

He replied, rather red in the face and in a hesitant manner "Because... because I am Doctor Harvard." He bowed his head down and I simply looked at him in shock.

"You're lying." I replied, followed by a short wheezy laugh.
"Am I? That's the thing about you English teachers, lovers of writing. You make up characters so well, you forget who is real and who is not. And for that matter, you forget *what* is real as well." He stared me up and down, remaining calm. This was one way to succeed in provoking an unpleasant reaction from me. He was succeeding.

He was laughing under his breath and looked up at me as though I was the most naïve woman he had ever met.

"Excuse me Miss...But it was not an accusation that you heard earlier in your class. I'm assuming that's why you're here? The words coming from that boy's mouth were accurate. I despise English and writing and this illusory concept that it can actually be considered a method of expression. Educational? Oh God. I mean, it's utterly ridiculous and I will continue to express my views." He looked at me, awaiting my reaction like his life depended on it. Well, I was not going to fulfil this expectation and satisfy an ignorant, narrow mind with my anger and exhaustion in trying to prove a point. So, I asked a question.

"Oh, I see. How interesting. And which aspect of this subject do you believe to be so pointless Doctor?" I maintained a serious expression with my eyes completely fixated on his entire being. He quickly became defensive as he stood up and started to pace the floors of his scientific palace of potentiality. It was like he was the God, the creator that bestowed the materials and equipment capable of performing wonders, exceeding all standard human logic. It made him feel powerful.

"Oh as a whole, I hate the subject. Furthermore, I refuse to believe that three, moaning, hysterical witches can predict a prophecy! Have you heard anything so ridiculous?" He paced further away now, down to the bottom of his laboratory, analysing in infatuation all types of strange devices which I dare not question.

"Oh, so you're familiar with Macbeth? I'm glad." I smiled a satisfactory smile.

"No. I'm familiar with women." He replied with the kind of seriousness expected from a comedian before the laughs come flooding in. It was clear that he was a very cynical man, but to add insult to injury, he was now a raging misogynist.

"Doctor Harvard... I would appreciate it if we kept our conversation focused on the subject of discussion rather than going off on a controversial tangent. Thank-you." I feigned a smile. It was the most awkward conversation I had ever had, with any teacher in the school. Surprisingly though, he interested me to the point where I wanted to know about him. I had to know about the reasons behind this well played out façade that was not only unattractive but obviously false.

"I see. Well, I do not believe there is anything else to discuss, so are we quite finished here Ms... I assume you're not married. Just seeking?" He questioned sarcastically.

I could feel now, the Goosebumps on my back and along my arms stiffen. My skin felt tight. Rage surfed carelessly along the ocean that was my bloodstream, waiting for that next big wave to present itself. And with that, the tsunami was complete.

"It's Ms, Ms Dakota. MS' NOT 'MISS' NOT EVEN 'MRS' ANYMORE. I'M A WIDOW GOD DAMMIT I'M A FUCKING WIDOW. DOESN'T ANYBODY GET THAT?! DOESN'T ANYBODY EVER THINK ABOUT ANYONE ELSE IN THIS WORLD OF SHIT?!!" I stopped as I saw this man's paralysed face. I couldn't help it. Suppression does something to a person. It changes every aspect of the personality and my change had now been made obvious, publicised to a man whom I barely knew. But it was too late, I had said too much and to be given the opportunity to reverse these actions would truly be miraculous.

A Doorstep Miracle

I shook and tried as best I could to stifle the tears that so desperately wanted to come out. I recovered soon enough, my tears dried and my shaking stopped. But I could never recover from what had been done and what I had kept locked up inside all this time just hoping for somebody to throw away the key so that I didn't have to hang onto it any longer. My 26 year old husband died 6 months ago at a community venue in Tennessee. He was beaten to death for expressing his views on racism, homophobia and other universal issues. He spoke about beautiful, inspiring things that really touched your heart. Sometimes when I listened to him, I felt so proud, so inspired. I was a part of his life and it made me proud. But he was taken from me, just like all good things.

Apparently it was a gang of older men from around town who had heard about what was going on at the venue, thought they might, as they said, well, as was reported written in the newspapers "put an end to this hippy, peace and harmony protest bullshit." They decided one day that they would take their anger out on my John. But that's not what John intended to do. He was placid and kind-hearted. All he ever wanted was to just open people's eyes, make them see that there was more to preconceptions, past traditions and discriminatory views that society had been indoctrinated by. He could have been someone great. Could have, would have, and should have.

Doctor Harvard stared and that's all he ever did. No signs of remorse. I suppose you could say that I wanted him to comfort me. Maybe you'd be right. But it was something about his silent observation alone that made it clear there was no need for words. I think he could see then that I had said all that I had to say. It wasn't even about the accusation anymore. We both knew that.

I left.

A Doorstep Miracle

I grabbed my keys and I left.

There were no consoling glances, not even an attempt.

I walked to my car and I did not look back. I couldn't look back. I spent the whole of the remainder of my life, just looking back. It was time to change the locks on the door of my past.

Today was what it was. It was a surprise and Lord knows life is just full of surprises. But I knew, everything happened for a reason. I met this man for a reason. That reason was yet to be deciphered.

Tomorrow was a brand new day, another day of mourning and pretending not to mourn. When my head hits that pillow, lord knows I'll be fast asleep and I can see John again in my dreams. That's the only place I ever saw him now, in my dreams.

2

Mission impossible?

It was 06:00 am and I had been woken by the sound of The Platters *'Only You'* playing next door, no doubt to the highest volume possible. Sometimes I believed my neighbours thrived off knowing they had annoyed me. But then that was probably due to my depressive state, or so the psychologists would say.

I went about my monotonous routine of sliding down the stairs, walking like a drunken lady over to the coffee and attempting, pathetically, to pour myself a cup. I then walked back upstairs with this cup of poorly made coffee and attempted to get dressed. I didn't care much for my hair anymore because I didn't care for anything anymore. I cared for John and I cared for my work, my countless unfinished novels I had told myself I would write. But he wasn't here anymore and I couldn't write anymore. He would have told me that I looked beautiful regardless. Sometimes you need that. Sometimes you forget that you are capable of being loved.

I brushed my teeth, tied my hair up and left, locking the door behind me.

My car looked just as worn out as I did. Rusty, deflated and generally depressed. He wasn't smiling like he usually did. John would always personify things. It was one of the many things I loved about him. He believed that everything was alive, that everything had a purpose beyond what we considered it to be, beyond what we knew it to be. He always tried to install a philosophy in me to never judge a book by its cover. But what happens, I wondered, when the book you have written or are writing

13

does not have a cover. Do people dismiss it? Ignore it? And what kind of cover would a book need to have, for it to be worthy of reading? I thought about Doctor Harvard. I wondered what book he would be but I wondered more so, what his cover would look like. The real cover.

I jumped in, started the ignition and drove off. Down that same road. John and I used to drive together down this road. Always this road. This road was the only road out of all near where we lived that appeared to go on for an eternity. I used to think that was what I wanted. But eternity now, was torturous. After staring into the distance of nothingness, I drove through and parked in the teacher's parking area. I sat for a few minutes just gathering myself. It was just another day, like the rest and although these days were different, I could still get through them. I had to, there was no other choice.

Life then presented itself to me in the most challenging of forms; simplicity. Life was so simple and already happening that it made it hard to feel and act normal. I felt as though the whole world should be crashing down and then Auden's 'Funeral Blues' came into my head almost like John had heard my thoughts. And although this was just a poem, the relevance of it could not have been more relevant if it tried. My world had stopped but the world as we all know it had not. It was like some kind of sick, twisted joke and everyone but I was in on it. Just like the classroom army was always in on it and I wasn't. Suddenly, I felt as though I were voluntarily participating as an extra in a sitcom, however, I was the joke, civilisation; the comedian, and the world; the spectator.

I got out of my car and walked into school in the same way, with the same view staring me in the face. I strolled into my classroom and sat. My class had already settled down and were burying their heads into those oh so well structured textbooks. Why couldn't life be a textbook?

"Ms… Hey Ms…You didn't speak to Dr Harvard yesterday did you?" Jed Waters give that familiar triumphant stare accompanied by a small, pathetic laugh. He exchanged a sad face expression with another class mate and motioned with is hands the act of crying. I took one glance at the class who were forcefully laughing. And I simply didn't have the strength left to tolerate any more.

"You know what? If my classes, wait no, if my presence bothers you so much that you have to make jokes about my job and therefore, my life, I couldn't even imagine where it is that you come from. In fact, I'm not sure if I even care. What kind of a person thrives off someone's misery? It's pathetic, you're pathetic. Your attempts to destroy me are futile. If only you knew what I'd been through in my life, your little attempts would be proven weak compared to the attempts that life has taken to knock me. Sit down in my classroom. You don't want to participate? Fine. But I will take great pleasure in watching those who want to, succeed and then you'll be Jed. Jed who?" I held my arms out wide. There was no laughter at all. Silence. Pure, tranquil, acknowledging silence.

Jed stared in shock and walked back to his place with no questions asked. Just as he did, there was a knock at the door. Everyone fell silent at the sight. It was Dr Harvard. I froze. Last night came back to me in blurred visions all at once. I knew how hard it must have been for him to come down here and be faced with everything he hated staring him in the face. I empathised with that because I could and I knew that our circumstances were different but nevertheless, that feeling I could see so evidently parading on his face with insouciance, that feeling, I felt that too.

"Dr … Harvard." I struggled to speak. It was like I was in the infantry stages of speech.

"Excuse me, I just needed a word." He whispered loudly. He appeared awkward and fragile. I didn't know whether this was because he was in this room on this department or whether he felt strange about my sudden outburst yesterday but I felt it. We both did.

The students' stared, puzzled with confusion at Dr Harvard's presence. He was a fish out of water, an alien in this territory and it became obvious very quickly.

"I… I'm rather busy teaching Doctor, perha—"I was then unexpectedly interrupted.

"I understand. I'll meet you in the cafeteria after your lesson? Or perhaps in my laboratory? "His eyes lit up hopefully. He stood, shaking with nerves and twitching.

"Urm, yes, perhaps, Doctor." I smiled politely and then turned myself away. This man was desperate, I could sense it, but for what?

He smiled back, confirming this. Then, he exited, closing the door behind him.

I hadn't realised it, but the time had passed so very quickly and it was nearly ten minutes until lunchtime. Had he done this purposely? Had this been all part of a plan? I grew paranoid beyond the point of sanity. My class read silently to themselves for the remainder of the lesson. Reading beautiful words. And all I could think about was yesterday in Doctor Harvard's laboratory. It was going to be challenging to revisit because when you revisit, you relive. This was a fact so real it was frightening. It was not only that one moment I would relive but in fact, it was rather like a chain reaction. Once an episode of emotions had been released, this would trigger another and I wasn't ready for that to happen yet. A friend once told me that to cry and to talk about things that had happened was the

but I ignored that. I had to. I wasn't about to let my weakness triumph this time.

He agreed to my condition, reluctantly but, nevertheless, he agreed.

"Well, I guess, I finished university. Got a job at one school, went to another. I didn't like the previous school. Their teaching methods were too unorthodox, I suppose you could say. I then discovered that I—"

"Doctor Harvard." I interrupted sternly with desperation in my voice.

"I meant your story. Not your educational history. I want to know about your real story, your life? No feigning. I want to hear about you right from the start. If we are going to do this, we're going to do it properly, agreed?" I stared until he stared back. I had to be sure that this man was telling the whole truth. He agreed with a reciprocal nod and a grunt.

"I see. Okay, well, let's see, ah. The youngest I can remember, would probably be, no doubt you'll enjoy this, in my English class. I had just been congratulated for a poem that I had written. We all had to do it. It was the sixth year at school and we had to do it for homework over the summer break. So, I was called to the front of the classroom. Everyone applauded, as you do. You're young. You don't exactly know what's going on and you simply imitate what everyone else is doing. So, there I read the abundance of words that I had come up with in an hour that previous night. As I was reading, I was rudely interrupted by two policemen who had walked into our classroom and…well, um…Um." There was a brief pause and Doctor Harvard had suddenly grown quiet. He fiddled with his tie and lab coat, like a fidgeting child urging to take their jumper off on sports day because of the overpowering heat. Beads of sweat developed rapidly on his forehead and he appeared extremely uncomfortable.

"Doctor, are you, are you alright?" I was genuinely shocked. I had so many things I could have said but their importance had quickly been marginalised. Words, the one thing I knew, I suddenly didn't know. I found myself now, without knowledge. And when words were insufficient, I resorted to physical contact. As I touched Doctor Harvard's hand, he squeezed it tightly, like I was his source of support.

With his head bowed slightly, it was hard to resume eye contact. But what I noticed, was the falling of tears from his eyes onto the table in front of us. They formed small puddles beneath his face and with a deep breath he lifted his head slowly with humiliation. I had never understood what men found so embarrassing about crying. But then, I realised that this was simply just another socially constructed idea with we were forced to comply with. Such a sad reality, I realise in moments like this. I had been through a lot in my life. I knew I did not appear to be the strongest women there was, but people didn't know me. And the things they had heard, didn't even come close to what was real. However, what I thought I was, whatever I believed my capabilities to be, I can say with the upmost sincerity that I was not prepared in the slightest, to sit here and watch this man who I assumed never cried, pour, literally, his heart out. I had witnessed a Doctor falling apart. What hope did we have? But then, he was only human, right? Whatever that meant anymore. I could feel that burning liquid filling up in my eye sockets again. I hated to cry. It shows weakness, my grandmother told me. But I remember that it hurt, seeing him hurting and with that, I couldn't abandon him ever.

"Doctor Harvard? What happened? You can tell me." I shook Doctor Harvard's arm, encouraging him to continue. But he wouldn't.

"I'm sorry." He said, snatching his arm away from my grip, leaving abruptly.

I was left, alone in the silence, sat in the same position I had been. I could not move. The production of tears was constant, as I came to the realisation that this man was more than what I thought he was. I felt so shallow for judging him before. I couldn't leave it there. I couldn't possibly just leave it there. It would be totally illogical. It would be like reading half way through a book and then starting a brand new one. I had to know what it was that was bothering him so much that he could not even bring himself to speak about it without suffocating in his thoughts.

I thought long and hard about the possibilities. Maybe he was scared of Policemen? Maybe he had terrible stage fright, it's very common. Even though these different reasons had come to my attention, it still played in the back of my mind that this man would not have been worried about things so manageable. He did not seem the sort of man to be particularly affected by petty problems such as this. Something extreme had happened on this day. I knew it. I could feel it in my guts. Something extreme enough to prohibit this man's creativity for years and I was going to discover what this was, even if it killed me, because, I was emotionally invested now and I was not the kind of person to abandon responsibility. I had John by my side and he was always watching over me. I knew of course he probably wasn't, but I took comfort in the thought anyway.

I made myself a promise that evening that I was going to do everything and anything in my power to help Doctor Harvard. And that is exactly what I intended to do.

3

The Yellow Card

This morning I woke up with the need to smoke. I went to the nearest convenience store and purchased a packet of Marlborough cigarettes. I came home. I sat. I stared in fascination at the tranquillity and stillness of the morning. It was beautiful. I couldn't help but feel this underlying guilt for carrying out a life-threatening act right in front of something so beautiful. It was ironic. I was staring, besotted with life being presented to me, and here I was, killing myself, jeopardising my life. It just seemed so wrong. I grabbed a Coffee and this time was functioning satisfactorily to pour it in the expected way that comes naturally to other human beings. No spillages, nothing wrong with the taste of the Coffee. Today was already going to be a good day, I just knew it. Lord, I deserved it. And so did Doctor Harvard. I thought about him all night. So much so, that at times I was kept wide awake just thinking about him crying. Anyone would have thought I was obsessed with him but, I just cared. I hadn't cared about someone for a while and it was therapeutic for me to care. It's what I used to be brilliant at. John always said I would have made an excellent mother because of how maternal and compassionate I was. I just cared about people, sometimes more than myself. It is, as I've been told, one of my many flaws. My father would often say to me that "people will take advantage of you. Once they've sensed your weakness, you're nothing. Like a coat on the hottest day of the year." But I was starting to think that if I didn't care for Doctor Harvard, and if he didn't care for himself, then who else would? I'd bet my whole life no one else cared about him and wanted to help him as much as I did in that moment when I held his hand.

A Doorstep Miracle

I noticed, as I stared thoughtfully out of the window, that in the reflection of the window, a small yellow card, with majestic red writing was gazing up at me. It read 'MS' and underneath in brackets written purposefully: (not Miss). It could only ever have been from one man. I smiled at this gesture. It had reminded me of all the sweet things that John used to do for me. He would spontaneously buy me flowers and lay them next to my bedside so that when I woke, they were the first thing I would see. It was important to him. He'd always say "start the day with a positive thought." And he was right, as usual. God I missed him. But what good was God now huh? It's like Stephen King said in 'The Green Mile', that when we say 'I don't understand' God replies, "I don't care." But it was getting easier now to remember the happiness I felt when I was with him, instead of remembering his body, lying there breathless and cold like some forgotten book on a shelf in an abandoned library, enduring the beginning stages of demolition.

So, with apprehension, I opened the letter. It was sealed with a kind of wax and stamped with a stencilled pattern. I felt like I had been invited to Hogwarts or somewhere grand like that. I thought long and hard about when he must have put it here on my desk. He left before me last night? How on earth would he have been allowed access to my classroom? Who knew? In fact, who cared? All I wanted to do was read this letter! It practically screamed to be opened. And so, with trembling hands, I slid my fingers underneath the envelope. I then tugged and the letter was opened. The wax peeling of slowly with it. I felt a sudden wave of hesitation passing through me, rather like when you were a kid, in the game of pass-the-parcel when the music stops. All eyes are focused on you and the pressure to tear off that next layer is unbearable.

The contents of the letter were folded up into quarters, with perfect symmetry (obviously). I didn't expect any less from Doctor Harvard. The paper was slightly thin, like that of the paper used in a bible. It was transparent, making it easy for me to notice two extremely long paragraphs. I pulled the letter out so that I could read it properly as, in this very moment, it appeared to be just an abundance of illegible words scrambled up on a piece of paper. But, as I pulled the letter out from the envelope in a vertical fashion, a smaller piece of paper fell out, landing slowly, like a feather, onto my shoe. It was slightly torn on the sides and looked old, tea stained and worn out. Forgetting the letter in hand, I bent down and picked this other letter of mystery up. It felt rusty and dry, like a preserved autumn leaf that had fallen. There was nothing on the side facing me, so my only other option was to turn it around and look on the opposite side. As I did, facing it to the sunlight, I noticed the words written in the most professional italic style. They stood out distinctly on the ruined paper. And my God, when I read what had been written, my heart sank. It was, you could literally say, a diamond in the rough. The words I had read, reduced me to tears.

"There was a young boy, he lived in Berlin,
He believed life itself was a sin.
He was so distraught that one day fought,
Fights with himself, but can't win.
He became so afraid,
Oh so dismayed when he knew no one could ever love him."

- ***James Harvard, year 6.***

I was speechless. It couldn't possibly be? Doctor Harvard? A young boy of this age believing in his heart that he amounted to nothing... it sickened me. Who had made him feel this way? I wanted to know who was responsible. It had to have stemmed from somewhere. But most of all, what I wondered the most, was why Doctor Harvard had not told me he could write! I mean, he obviously had the talent. Did he do this on purpose? To prove a point to me that he could write, but just hated it for the sake of hating something. I wondered.

In all of this sudden confusion, like some beacon of hope, a sense of love was restored in me after reading this, purely because I then remembered what it was that made me want to become a writer. From simply reading these six lines, I felt like I knew everything about this man, I felt his raw, indestructible emotion. No hospital document, personal reference or passport could ever have told me this much about a person. Because these were simply, numerical, statistical facts and opinions. But when one writes, it does not get more real than that. When one writes, it is their heart they publicise, the real truth about their journey to hell and back along with their ticket as evidence and lord did I feel the darkness now. When you write, you are no longer a statistic, you are no longer and opinion. You are an individual soul. Writing tells the truth, the whole truth and nothing but the truth.

When I had finished sobbing to myself rather pathetically, it had dawned on me that I had temporarily abandoned the additional document on my desk. I had to retrieve it. Maybe, this document would provide this one with some clarity. I unfolded it carefully, with precision to ensure that I didn't damage or rip what I believed to be an ancient artefact.

"Dear Ms (Not Miss) Dakota, I apologise for yesterday evening, however, I feel rude considering the mutual agreement that we had, if I were not to explain myself in some way. I must admit, it is not my preferred method of communication, however, I feel I cannot speak about the incident verbally. I fear that speaking shall only contribute to the unbearable pain I feel when expressing my emotions on the matter. I hope you understand as, I'm sure you will.

A Doorstep Miracle

I know you will understand as a teacher of the subject that writing my story would be a far better expression compared with the constant pauses due to the stifling of determined tears. I fully appreciate the time you will have taken out of your schedule to read this, if you have at all but similarly, I understand if you have no interest in investing your time in this letter due to my previous hostility towards you. For that I also apologise. Social awkwardness I have been told is one of my many flaws along with my disastrous dress sense.

Ms Dakota, when I as eleven years of age, I wrote a poem, the very one that you hopefully received and are probably holding in your hands at this very moment. As I was saying yesterday evening, I was going to read this poem out to my classmates but was interrupted by two policemen. These policemen were not, as one would assume, here for a school assembly, or for show and tell. These people, ones whom society invests their trust, were the individuals that informed me that my life, as I knew it, was about to change forever. My parents had been victims of a serious car accident. Killing them instantly. Of course it did not register at first. I was young, and if I am being completely honest with you, it still does not register when I think about it. And this is why I do not. My parents were extremely respected people. Very strict. My father was a renowned Doctor and my mother, a mathematician. They met at Cambridge University and from then on, as I've heard, were inseparable. I feel awful speaking of them this way, however, it must be said; I was supressed by the life they had chosen for me. The expectations were too high and I was scared that my inabilities would prevent me from fulfilling them. All I ever wanted to do was to live, to travel mostly. I saw no point in education, and after that day, I saw no point in writing anymore. Every time I saw a poem, a book, an English classroom, that day would come back to haunt me again. It was… it still is unbearable. As a result, I became contemptuous towards both parents and

26

I had theorised that they resented me for my creativity. No matter how much they wanted it, I was never going to be their perfect child. I didn't blame them really, for, I do not think highly of myself Ms, actually, I feel very lowly of myself. I am not happy and I am not sad. I am within and without. Simply waiting. I was forced then to grow up quickly and before I knew it, my life was living more than I was. I knew I had to pay tribute to my father in some way, I felt obligated to do so. So, I learned about physics, other sciences, researched from his notes and from other recommended materials. I became a Doctor and I decided I wanted to teach this to other young people who wanted to know about it. I felt like a disciple of Jesus, spreading the word of God to all of his willing listeners. I have been here for two weeks now and then I met you, although, I wish I'd had the chance to meet you all over again.

I hope this provides you with some kind of clarity.

Regards,
Doctor James Harvard.

The letter was deeply touching. It provided me with some clarity on the poem and gave me some information about why Doctor Harvard was the way he was. But I knew there was more to the story than that. I could feel its insufficiency radiating. But, I also understood how much this must have taken for him to write emotionally and so I wasn't going to push him for any more answers. For now, I had to settle with a partial truth. I suddenly thought, are we all just partial truths? Do you ever really, completely know someone? Or is this an illusion we kid ourselves with as a consolation, a substitution for our fear of loneliness? One day, I would know everything there was to know about this man. It was my mission (other than marking essays and embarking on usual teacher duties) but I was hooked now. The addictive nature of not knowing, held me in its tight grip and I desired to know more. I thought that maybe, if I got him to write, eventually, if he ever wrote again, would this tell me more? I wondered and I couldn't stop. This man was my enigma now and the codes had yet to be deciphered.

After minutes sitting in silence, I decided to grab some paper and a pen and write a response. The very thought of revisiting my past scared me to the point where I struggle to pick the pen up. I stared at it. Staring in contemplation and questioning myself. Was I really going to do this? Put myself through this again for someone who I knew but didn't know? The thought frightened me like a ghost. But sometimes ghosts are not friendly animations, cartoons or masks worn on Halloween. Sometimes, they are the thoughts that saunter insouciantly in your head whilst your struggle goes unnoticed. Sometimes, you can be haunted without being thrown against the wall by a deadly spirit or by being taunted by strange noises in your home. Sometimes it is simply being that is haunting. Your body becomes a home in which these things inhabit and before you know it, demolition is impossible; your fate is concreted like the foundations of a home and you'll never escape.

Doctor Harvard,

Thank-you for your letter. I found it both deeply touching and yes, thank you, the poem provided some clarity. My story, I can tell you now will not be one that interests you, but one I believe may only contribute to your grief. I know as one of its critics, it could do with some work...

That was it. I couldn't continue. I was broken already. And as the ghosts laughed at my weakness, my body grew incapable. My pencil dropped. They were taking my ability away. My thing, the thing I was good at. Everybody has a thing and that was mine but I feared it was now to be acquired by some omnipotence that I could not explain nor comprehend.

I gasped for air. Something was killing me and I needed to murder it before it murdered me.

I would not be replying to Doctor Harvard's letter, as, my response was both weak and unsatisfactory. Not up to the standards of an English Teacher in the slightest. The man was owed more than that. So, I would find him and I would speak to him. I would try to help him, and if that didn't work, then I would find another way. There was always another way. And I would be lying if I were to say that in attempting to fix Doctor Harvard that I wasn't trying to fix myself. Because truly I did not know how I would or even could fix myself but I knew that investing my patience in someone else would enlighten me on what I needed to do to help my situation.

I got in my car a little while after and I drove home not even paying attention to the Road and the things I may have killed in my endeavour to arrive home as quickly as possible. When I arrived home, I just sat for a minute. I sat and I waited and there it was again. The tears that pushed their way out of my eyes like a party trick, ready to perform for a non-existent audience. I tried, God I tried so damn hard to prevent them from flowing down my cheeks. I tried to distract myself, and so, I decided that maybe music was the best option I had here. Perhaps this was all I needed to calm me down. I had blamed it on the day that I had had and especially the incident that occurred earlier. Music helped and at times I considered it a type of therapy. Not like writing though. Oh God no, never like writing. Not a thing on earth could compare to that feeling of home when my hands grabbed that pen and started writing. Sometimes I couldn't stop and would develop blisters on my fingers from the tightness of my grip. It was like some strange, inexplicable type of magic and I knew all of the tricks because I was my own magician.

A Doorstep Miracle

I rummaged through the CD box in the back of my car and I couldn't find anything remotely interesting. But what I saw in the corner of my eye was much more interesting. I was simultaneously excited and scared to death to pick this CD up and play it. It was mine and John's mix-tape. We made it in the summer together just before he had died and all of our favourites were on there. I contemplated to pick it up. It was the most difficult decision I had ever made and although it may seem ridiculous, it was all I had left of him. All that remained of my previous life. The pain was one that reminded me of a child when they remember how traumatic their first injection at the doctor's was. It hurt, and that stuck, so they never wanted to go through it again. I didn't want to go through it again but I did at the same time and it was a contemplation that amounted to agony. As I stared, my breath increased and I could feel in sporadic torrents, waves of nervousness manifesting in the very pit of my stomach.

Reaching out and then hesitating, I stopped, shaking for some time. And with that, I grabbed the CD, opened it violently and inserted the disc into the CD player with considerable force. There was silence. There was silence and then there was the sound of something indicating an electrical fault. With that I went to eject the disc because there was no point in trying anymore. It simply wasn't going to work and I couldn't do anything about it. Just as I reached out to press the eject button, the most beautiful, almost sacred sound came to my ears and projected itself around the confines of my ruined car. It was Jeff Buckley's *'Hallelujah'*, the first song on the disc. As it played the hairs on my arms and the ones that ran vertically down my neck were standing infallibly. I was paralysed. My breathing had temporarily stopped, along with the movement in my face and limbs and all at once I thought the beating of my heart would stop also. It seemed the only thing proving that I was still alive was the falling of my tears that told me I was not dead, not truly.

I let out one breath of release and then inhaled just as quickly as I had exhaled. This only fuelled my breathing pattern to complicate more, ending in a series of short, hard breaths which then of course resulted in me crying uncontrollably. I had never before known what people meant when they claimed that they 'couldn't stop. I just couldn't stop', not until now. Because I really couldn't stop, I just couldn't stop. My head lost all stability and whacked onto the steering wheel, again with considerable force, but I didn't feel it, not one little bit. I would feel it in the morning just like I felt everything else; in the morning.

And so, I sat and I turned the volume up so that the beauty of the music drowned out my thoughts. I was utterly alone and at one with music. I felt John there by my trembling side and so achingly longed to feel his warm touch on the edge of my shoulder. That touch of consolation that always seemed to settle me in moments of dismay and seemingly endless disaster.

The song had ended. So had this eternal mourning. It had to stop now. I had let it get the better of me for too long and it had succeeded in devouring the very core of who I was. But then I realised, it was who I *was*, who I used to be and who I cannot be anymore. Something had to change and when my head rose from that steering wheel I had a good feeling about this life, about this possibility. The book of my previous life, riveting, immensely youthful and without any doubt, the most amazing narrative one could ever tell, yet, it was time to put this book down. It was time to pick up another book and start reading about where my new life would take me. I realised that now and all I wanted to do, all I ever wanted to do was to fix it. To fix myself, and maybe, just maybe I would succeed in fixing Doctor Harvard too.

4

A second chance

It is not every day that you meet someone who truly intrigues every ounce of your being. As I stared in the mirror the next morning, I began to think about it more and more. Are the first impressions we make, definitions of ourselves without conscious realisation? Are we simply the pretend versions of ourselves when we are actively being who we think is us? I thought about my first impression with Doctor Harvard and of what I thought about him that day when I met him outside of the laboratories.

Was that really him?

Was that really me?

The real me, would have never gone down there in the first place. I would have let the accusation slide, not giving a shit because my husband had just died and I wasn't thinking straight. Was that who I was pretending to be? Was that who society wanted me to be? Because the day I met Doctor Harvard, the truth came out. Unexpectedly, but nonetheless, it came out. I had introduced who I was trying to supress, screaming and crying. That whole vulnerable persona had vanished and I was a fierce, nasty, unapproachable bitch. But that was me, right? Then I realised we're all supressed in one way or another. There is no escaping it and indeed if it becomes too powerful, there is no other option but to let the catharsis happen. But although I had made this impression, I was not satisfied with it. I was going to give Doctor Harvard that 'second chance' that he had wished for in his letter and I was going to do it for myself too. Then I realised, we all deserve a second chance… right?

As I walked through the school corridors, I felt a sense of beginning. Something new was going to happen and change had never been more welcome. It was change that ruined me and change that promised me recovery, resurrection, freedom.

I spied Doctor Harvard amongst the noise of the adolescent jungle in a cold, clinical appearing cafeteria. He sat with an eating tray, a carton of orange juice, peas, carrots and a strange looking concoction of spaghetti shapes piled on top of a lump of stone, cold potato. His head was bowed and he sat slumped over his meal in his enormous, heavy lab coat that reminded me of an oppressive grey cloud hanging over the city in the sky. The cafeteria smelt of a multiplicity of contrasting perfumes and foods. It was that high school smell that you can never really forget even if you try. Nostalgia to the nostrils.

I strolled over to Doctor Harvard in what felt like slow motion. Suddenly I was back in high school, I was seventeen and walking over to meet John. This flash back occurred so frequently, in and out of what was a dream and of what was real. It disorientated me slightly but I was fine. I walked to his table and stood, hitting the side of it slightly. Enough to dodge his tray and make it slide half way down the other end of the table. He first stared at my shoes and then worked his way up slowly. He flinched, fidgeting with the frames of his thin glasses with trembling hands. It was as awkward for me as it was for him. He probably felt rejected as I had not yet replied to his letter or should I say, death certificate. And I, well, I felt shame for not replying sooner or for that matter replying at all. And when starring him in the face, there was an evident, mutual embarrassment. His cheeks were a deep read, like he was suffering with fever. Mine, similar. Very similar. I opened my mouth to try and form a sentence and failed. At once, he looked down in disappointment which only made me want to attempt again.

"Doctor Harvard. I believe I have still to respond to your letter." I stood, maintaining full eye contact, although, he struggled with that, a lot.

"Oh, the letter, I totally forgot about that." He muffled a response under his breath and acted like he was oblivious to the whole affair. His head was still bowed in shame like a child that is being told off by their parents.

"Doctor Harvard, please. I had the intention of replying sooner, but. Well, the truth is, is that the subject is quite a sensitive one. I feel awful for saying this because of what I read in your letter…uh, I just." I paused again, not knowing quite how to word it. I feel that if I spoke anymore, I would just exceed the boundaries of human decency.

"Sit down." Doctor Harvard instigated by kicking the seat opposite him with his foot. I immediately sat, feeling vulnerable and nervous.

"I'm assuming you want to give me your sympathy so that I feel better and that you will then feel better because that is what happens when people give other people sympathy. They feel better for giving it. Well, if that is truly all that you came to do, Ms, I can tell you now with honesty, I do not need it. I do not require any more sympathy from anyone else. I have had enough and it is now a chore to receive it. To thank people for giving it out like it is a cup of tea or a packet of tissues. I am quite done, Ms.Dakota. And I understand if you do not want to tell me your story, but I am simply disappointed. I had a feeling it would have been interesting. But never mind. Good day, Ms." He smiled that obligatory smile and continued to eat his meal.

I was silent for quite some time and I spent this time just staring. Analysing what he was doing. I watched him eating his food, I watched the way he piled it onto the cutlery like it was all part of a routine. But I knew he didn't want to eat. I knew he didn't want to sleep. I knew he probably couldn't sleep. I knew this because I had been there and I had felt like that to. There is nothing more powerful than empathy.

"Doctor Harvard!" I shouted, although not loud enough for the students to hear. But I made Doctor Harvard jump. He dropped both his knife and fork immediately. Tears formed in my eyes like tiny beads of a beautiful necklace and an immovable lump in my throat I feared would prevent me from speaking in a time where it was of the upmost importance.

"Doctor Harvard. I need to tell you my story. I must tell you my story. That is what I was trying to tell you just now but I cannot speak. It hurts to speak." I shrugged, laughing at myself and staring him in the face as I was speaking. He could comprehend the desperation on my face.

"Doctor, would you just come with me. Come for a coffee. Come to my house, for a coffee? I must tell you about me." I attempted to smile, but tears rolled down my cheeks and made it impossible to smile sincerely. I spent a few seconds wiping them away. My voice was now a faint whisper in comparison to the shouting. I simply couldn't speak. It became an unmanageable task. I buried my head in my hands to conceal this weakness that I had yet again publicised.

"I accept your offer." Doctor Harvard spoke softly.

A Doorstep Miracle

I took my hands from my face and stared at him. I laughed a small laugh of relief with tears still falling. I mimed to him the words 'thank you' with which he reciprocated a small smile that said 'it's okay, I know what you're going through and I also know you're going to be okay.'

It was then that I realised that in this world, although there are wars and conflicts that affect the entire world, there are also bigger wars. There are microcosmic wars, the wars in our heads that we cannot nor do not understand how to fight.

5

The power in being powerless

And it was so, that Doctor Harvard and I were the only humans in my living room. With hearts beating, inhaling and exhaling the shared oxygen. Sharing the pain that we had both experienced, trying to fight a war of which we had both become victims.

I boiled the kettle and lightened the mood by putting *'The Smiths Greatest Hits'* CD on lightly. Although I was American, I had always admired English music and I knew Doctor Harvard being English himself would appreciate this. His eyes brightened up when he heard Morrissey's voice and a look of astonishment appeared on his face. It was as though he couldn't believe that I listened to this kind of music. But then, no one is what they seem, I have realised.

His face particularly lit up when *'Hand in Glove'* came on. He smiled like he could trace back to when he had first heard this song and to who he had known and even to where he was. Something in him was dancing, even if it wasn't physically obvious. Something was. It was the happiest I think I'd seen him in the little time that I'd known him and that in itself spoke words which he couldn't. I smiled at him and then asked him if he wanted a cup of Tea. He agreed he did and so I went to make it.

Once the kettle had boiled, I came back with of cups of Tea.

"Thank you, Ms Dakota." He took the cup carefully, trying not to spill any anywhere.

A Doorstep Miracle

"It's alright, I hope you like no sugar. I seem to have fallen short. I've been, you could say, rather busy." I smiled, stifling my tears with a developing lump forcing itself up my windpipe, making this hard to manage. I had to put a brave face on I figured. But then, I figured this would be quite the manageable task considering I had been doing it for the past 6 months.

"It's quite alright Ms Dakota. I do not take sugar anyway." He replied and sipped his Tea contently.

There was an atmosphere of silence as we waited for the next song to play. We both knew that there were things to discuss. There were wars to be won. I was simply trying to find the courage to embark on the journey down memory lane. Procrastination was always a strength of mine. Finally though, the words managed to fall out of my mouth, although, rather reluctantly at that.

"Doctor Harvard, I suppose I should begin with my story." I spoke nervously and tried to disguise my fear by sipping more Tea. This way I didn't have to speak and simply couldn't.

"I suppose so." He smiled and held his Tea cup up in a celebratory fashion with his arm and index finger pointing up to the ceiling. Although, I knew it was a sarcastic gesture to break the tension. I laughed. Sometimes laughter helps, but sometimes it isn't enough.

"Okay, well, I suppose I should start with how I got here, in this job, in this city. I was a young 13 year old girl and I lived in the most pleasant neighbourhood you could imagine. It was sunny and the people were jolly, as much as they could ever be. I had the best friends, the best family. There were no mistakes made, nothing that jeopardised that. That was until…Sorry. That was -- until. It was a dark night in November and I was having the best night of my life. Everyone was ecstatic. Alcohol was rolling in and the people were continuously dancing. My parents were in the back garden." I paused and felt that chocking sensation again, consuming me like I was drowning. Drowning in everything like I had been for the months that passed since John.

"Ms. Dakota. Please, I am very patient when I try. Please do not rush yourself. I have time." Doctor Harvard grabbed my hand and squeezed it tightly. This only made me want to throw myself at him and fall apart like I had done in his laboratory. But I couldn't do that, could I? It wasn't acceptable, was it? What on earth would society say? A teacher holding responsibility for entire classes, planning lessons, paying rent, whilst simultaneously grieving for her dead husband. A breakdown? Oh no! Don't be silly…she simply isn't under ENOUGH stress. She would most likely have to succumb to the pressures of her suicidal tendencies to even be considered as someone how MAY have a breakdown.

"If you do not interpret this the wrong way, Ms, it seems from what knowledge I do know, that you have succumbed to what many refer to when referring to the emotional sector of the brain, as, well… you show the conventional symptoms causing one to, well, fall apart." Doctor Harvard was staring at me now with focused eyes and a firm grip that promised the world in that moment.

With that it was done.

I had broken down, completely and there was nothing I could do about it once it had begun. And as I was crying on Doctor Harvard, pouring my heart out to him, I could feel him crying too. I felt his chest convulse and in that moment it was clear that we were both falling apart. But in that moment of weakness, I had never felt more powerful. I embraced pain like a family member. I revelled in it. The dark staining liquid of melancholy that can never be washed out.

And so we held each other.

We held each other tightly for a while.

Strangers that were now friends.

Comfort in pain.

Once exhausted, once recovered temporarily, we sat, sipping our Tea and listening to *'The Smiths'*. Everything was normal again, for the moment. We were normal people, with normal problems living normal lives. It was a comforting charade.

"Your father hit your mother. You saw. You couldn't believe that your life had been so well pretended. You didn't want to believe that your life had been so well disguised with an image of how it is all supposed to be. And so you write, because there, you can write a story about how it is all supposed to be and no one can tell you that it is wrong because you can just say that it is fiction, yes?"

Doctor Harvard stared at me with swollen eyes from where he had been crying. The son of a bitch was right. The night I saw my father hit my mother, what did I do? Damn right, I wrote about it. It was the first thing that came to me. It had never left me since. It never would. It was both a blessing and a curse but one thing it did for me, was open my eyes. It opened my imagination to other worlds, other people, and other outcomes. One night, I wrote about an outcome that I had imagined. One that wasn't what I had seen and one that promised I would never see anything like that again.

"Yes. Yes, you are right Doctor Harvard. But then, I knew that. You knew that." I said, calmly followed by a friendly smile.

He laughed, wiping his face. I had never really seen how alluring his eyes were until they were exposed to the natural light.

"Doctor Harvard, what beautiful eyes you have!" I marvelled.

"All the better to see you with, my dear." He replied, laughing as he did so. There was a mutual laughter as I was reminded of the fairy-tale he was referring to.

All of the Tea had ran out and all we had was the remainder of songs yet to play on *'The Smiths'* CD.

"I've always loved The Smiths they remind me of my adolescent days." Doctor Harvard smiled pleasantly.

"I have loved them since I moved out. It was once when I was in England visiting an old friend that I had come across this abstract sound, with a voice that was so distinct. I admired it. I bought the CD straight away." I smiled and held it close to my chest.

Silence prevailed again.

"Doctor Harvard. I can help you." I said, all jokes aside, with the upmost solemnity.

What makes you think I need helping?" He asked, confused and defensive, pursing his lips profusely after taking a small, pointless sip of his Tea. It must have gone cold. He hated being offered help and his pride made that clear.

A Doorstep Miracle

"I don't know, perhaps, the fact that we have just sat here and cried together for over half an hour. Perhaps that may be one reason? Or have I simply just imagined the past half an hour?" I raised my eyebrow, starting at him intently. He looked up with guilty eyes and stared back at me for a while.

"Okay. Maybe I could use a little advice but not…help." He grunted, fiddling with his fingers that were now childishly knotted like laces on a pair of abandoned trainers.

"Doctor Harvard, it's okay to admit that you've had enough, you know. I don't think you're weak. If you're weak then only God knows what I am. You need help and it's okay to admit that." I touched his hand comfortingly and resumed to stare at him until he got the message.

He smiled reluctantly as though smiling were a task painful beyond belief. Suddenly, he flinched, the mood changed drastically and he strolled over to the CD player with rage, turning Morrissey's alluring voice off (this upset me greatly). I tried to appear nonchalant, insouciant and cool like a confident journalist but I couldn't maintain this for very long.

"So go on then! What help is it that you can offer Ms? Or should I say Doctor Dakota!" Doctor Harvard spoke sternly, with rage seeping from the pores in his face and I don't mean in a metaphorical sense either. I mean, the veins in his forehead were dilated to the highest degree possible. So much so, I was anticipating at any moment for his head to explode completely. His tone was cold and sarcastic, although, I'd expected this of course. It was the most obvious sign telling me that someone was in denial; defensiveness. This guard he'd been putting up for years was finally breaking. But it wasn't enough. I wanted to see him fall apart. It was the only way I could even attempt to build him back up again.

"Doctor Harvard. I may not be God, I may not have a PHD in physics or know the secrets behind the inner workings of the heart and mind but what I do have is experience. I know what it is to hurt and I know how to hurt others and what's more is I know how to channel it. Nothing is more powerful than experience. I can offer you a medicine. One that has no specified dose to be taken, one that far exceeds standardized moderation." I am almost at the point of tears but try to stifle it with a series of feigned coughs.

There is silence for a while and all that is audible is the ticking of my clock.

"Please, Ms. Dakota. I beg of you, do not mock me. Not now I have told you so much." His eyes released a glare of despair and he sat slumped with his head in his hands.

"But I would never do that. I could never do that to you. Do you understand me?" I bent down to his eye level and although I could not see his eyes, I knew he was listening to me.

He took his hands away from his eyes that were now red-rimmed and puffy. He had been crying even more. His eyelashes had on then fragments of tears that were sticking, making it appear, rather amusingly, like he was wearing mascara. I smirked at the thought and to this, his face frowned.

"What on earth could possibly be so entertaining in this moment?" He said quietly with a serious, emotionless face.

"Nothing, it's just that…well, oh don't worry. You looked like you had mascara on for a second there. Excuse me." I

43

blushed a deep red, hoping he was going to forget about what I had just said but to my surprise, he laughed, wiping his eyes profusely.

"Oh, goodness me. I didn't realise. How humiliating." He smiled, rubbing his face even harder now.

Doctor Harvard, it's quite alright. I believe to truly cure your ills, you must write. There is truly no other medicine available, more sufficient, and more reliable than this. You must write." I grabbed both his hands tightly, cupping them together. The proximity between us closer than it could ever have been. It dawned on me suddenly for just a minute that I have not known this man for very long and in fact, for that matter, I do not really know him at all. Could he unexpectedly switch on me? Harm me? There were endless possibilities entering my mind. It was then that I realised the stupidity of these suggestions. It was then, that I realised how beautiful a thing it is to get to know someone. To open up to them as if you were the only souls on this earth. No questions asked, no anxiety felt. Just two people, two broken hearts, four desperate hands and a ticking clock.

Doctor Harvard looked up into my eyes, properly, for the first time ever and I will never, so long as I live, forget what he said to me in that moment.

"Help me." He whispered with desperation.

There are no words that are worthy of being used to describe the emotions, the sheer relief that I felt in this one, simple moment. I saw Doctor Harvard as the protagonist of his own story (much to his annoyance). I saw a man, once superior, fall weak to the inevitability of life; the antagonist. It was the most beautiful moment. To see a person stripped naked of all facades, of all pretences, to see a person simply just be, I was in awe of him. I was in awe of the courage he had to break down and it scared me. It scared me beyond imagination because I knew I couldn't do it myself. I didn't possess the capability. I was weak. But in Doctor Harvard's weakness, sitting there, powerless, he was the most intimidating, most powerful HUMAN I had ever seen. He was human, so, so human that it was anomalous.

My tears fell, shamelessly and unrestrained. All I could manage was a nod to let him know that this was an offer I was going to accept unconditionally. Doctor Harvard, or should I say, James Harvard, was now a friend. We had connected in a moment of mutual defeat but things were going to change now. They were going to change for the better and I was going to do whatever I could in my power to make sure this happened.

"On one condition." Doctor Harvard said challengingly. I cocked my head to the side, as, I was momentarily confused about his request, about what it could be.

"What do you mean Doctor Harvard?" I stared, wide-eyed and puzzled.

"Let me help you, also." He stared, smiling enthusiastically like he was about to embark on the next revolutionary project that had been postponed temporarily. He held his hand out, instigating some sort of physical contract. And with that, I feebly reached out my hand. He grabbed it immediately, shaking it firmly. This made things official. Let the lessons begin. Let the war be won.

6

Ms Dakota's Lesson One: Similes and Metaphors

"Doctor Harvard! Please, sit, sit!" 'I shouted ecstatically. He walked in slowly, smiling sarcastically. In his hand were simply a pen and one sheet of paper.

"Ms Dakota, enlighten me." He waved his arms above his head satirically, to which I gave a sigh with the inkling of a laugh in it.

"I shall do my very best Doctor." I smiled, holding my books and pen up with enthusiasm.

I wrote on the board with a board marker in bold, capital letters 'SIMILIES AND METAPHORS.' I turned to witness Doctor Harvard's reaction. His facial expressions were, as I expected contemptuous and uncooperative. Already I knew that this was going to be harder than I had initially anticipated but this was not going to change anything. I wasn't going to allow it to dent my determination. Perhaps I would attempt a different, more unorthodox approach to my teaching. Yes, I would try this. Hopefully he would co-operate if I were to establish more coherently the conditions of *this* experiment. We would play it his way. We would, putting what I preach into practise, pretend that this lesson was an experiment. Perhaps he would feel more at ease or more in his element with this approach. Well, there was only one way to find out.

"Doctor. I feel I've thrown you in at the deep end. Perhaps we could try an alternative approach to this lesson?" I suggested with a hopeful look in my eye. He stared at me, curious and concentrated, stroking his chin in the most peculiar fashion, just as the scientists do on television shows.

"Hmm. What was it you had in mind, Ms Dakota?" He mumbled, with a microscopic sense of optimism hidden in his voice.

"Well…" I stopped speaking. Maybe this was too risky. Perhaps he may take it to offense if I suggested my idea. I grabbed my board marker and tried to draw what I meant, whilst explaining quickly so that there was next to no chance of an inquisition.

"Doctor Harvard. What if I said that writing were a science? The required devices such as similes and metaphors were in actual fact, simply the required elements ensuring that the experiment was fair?" I shrugged knowing in the back of my mind that an objection was about to be fired at me immediately. Strangely, I was wrong.

"Hmm. Interesting. Do continue Ms Dakota." His eyes were engaged now and he appeared startlingly interested in my method.

"Oh… yes. Well, consider writing temporarily, as a science? With the necessary conditions, you will achieve the desired results when following the hypothesis, method, equation if you like." I was becoming more enthusiastic now and I believed truly for the first time in a long time that progress was being made.

Doctor Harvard's face suddenly resembled that of a three year old in awe of a brand new toy. It was as though, you could say, he had experienced the eureka moment that every ambitious scientist strives for.

"So, your hypothesis is that writing is a type of science? An experiment complying fairly with required conditions in order to achieve fair results... tell me more Ms Dakota." Usually, I would be able to identify the introductory signals of Doctor Harvard's sarcasm revealing itself. However, this time, I truly saw in his face that he was thoroughly interested. No sarcasm detectable and for the first time, I was starting to enjoy my job again. It was great to feel appreciated for once. When did being truly listened to become a privilege? I had felt...since John...I had felt, well, I had felt undervalued, supressed, reclusive and above all, invisible. But when I saw that spark in Doctor Harvard's eye, that spark that says 'this is me. I like this, this is what I live for' the familiarity of that look was restored in me by the glimpse of his face. In that moment, I loved again, passionately, what I felt was previously impossible. I wanted to teach, I wanted to learn, and I wanted to feel... again and again just like I had before.

"I'm elated that you're interested! Doctor, this could be it! Don't you see? Combining our knowledge together? It's a synergetic breakthrough." I smiled, my teeth revealing themselves. My lips were now stretched so far apart, I was afraid they might tear.

He smiled at me, still in the midst of concentration.

"Mm, yes. Perhaps, Ms Dakota, perhaps." His smile faded slightly and for a second I could only assume that he was recollecting that day. The day when writing and everything about its beauty became that of a torturous scar, imprinted on his heart with a burning hot poker. It tugged on my heartstrings and for a moment, I was scared that I had become too involved with this man. I was now emotionally invested in everything. He had informed me of everything. With this knowledge I intended, even with the smallest of attempts to help this man. And so I pressed on relentlessly.

"Don't you see Doctor? The similes and metaphors are the conditions to abide by. The combination of these conditions with the core meaning of the written subject, is the experiment. The result is the quality of this combination, the quality of this expression and the quality of the idea behind the written piece." By this point, I was slamming my hands down profusely on my desk, waltzing around my classroom seeking an object with which I could throw at Doctor Harvard so that sense would eventually travel from that heart of his and into his brain so that he could marvel at the potential of this idea. "At least let me try Doctor? At least attempt it yourself? I will help you. Remember, you're never on your own…James." I walked slowly over to Doctor Harvard, squeezing his hand and gazing at him directly in the eyes. His eyes. His eyes, empty and holding the potential to be filled up with new ideas, new beginnings and revolutionary changes. But instead, momentarily, all that was filling them, were the tears of a broken soul, wounded beyond repair and trying his hardest to escape from the suffocating wall of pessimism which had built itself in the absence of his optimism.

He gave me that same, eternal gaze of desperation and whispered feebly, like he had done before, "Help me." I felt a pins and needles sensation as the squeezing of my hand grew tighter. I was unaware of him even holding it in his grasp. I was surprised and stunned that a man so introverted and seemingly weak could temporarily stop all circulation in my hand, causing it to turn an unnatural shade of purple mixed with blue. I didn't mind though. As long as he had released what feeling he had to, cathartically, I was satisfied. Oh, I would help Doctor Harvard until the very end of his life if I were given the opportunity.

"I will." I replied, still, maintaining his eternal gaze passively. It was like I absorbed his pain for those seconds. I saw into the depths of his pain and of his grief and for one second I was the one to take that pain away for him. I wanted to feel that again. I wanted to be the one to take that pain away. Not just for a second. This time, I would take it away permanently. I knew that this was the right thing to do because, it was simple. Seeing him hurt, it made me hurt.

I returned to the whiteboard and continued to write. We would start first with defining the terms. This would provide Doctor Harvard with the tools to then use these terms within sentences.

"Doctor Harvard..." I said, ready to start.

"James." He insisted.

"James. Right. So, James, I don't want to patronise you but we are going to be learning about what metaphors and similes are today." I smiled a comforting smile.

"Oh...really? I would never have guessed." Doctor Harvard smiled that smile that says 'I am trying to piss you off, you know that right?'

"James. I would prefer it if you toned down the sarcasm when in my classroom." I giggled. This was amusing. For once, I was the one who knew it all and Doctor Harvard was the pupil, yet to become educated.

"Well, Ms Dakota, I disagree. Is it not true that life is the teacher and humanity, the student?" He grinned when he saw my eyes widen with interest and positivity. I grinned back, elated.

"That was... that was brilliant!" I grinned jumping and clapping my hands.

"Thank-you, Ms" he grinned, nodding triumphantly.

"Carrie." I insisted.

There was a brief silence and words were not needed to explain the peace of the moment. It was simply tranquil and understanding, like an old friend.

"So, you are beginning to like the subject?" I asked, playing nervously with my hands again.

"I am beginning to find it easier to tolerate." Doctor Harvard stared down at his sheet of paper. I smiled, for, I knew he wished to confess his interest in the subject but his pride prevented him from doing so. He reminded me of my grandfather. Stubborn and strong-minded.

"I trust that I'm a student promised success due to the result of that individual experiment?" Doctor Harvard gazed up at me with eyes that laughed.

"Well, I don't know about being the most successful student, however, it could be promised that you are the most distracting." I stared back, exchanging a reciprocal glance of laughter.

"James, I am going to set you some homework, if you don't mind?" I flicked through some extra reading excitedly.

"Well, then on the subject, Ms Dakota. I have some research that you need to attend to. It needs to be bought to my lessons in order for you to participate with the lesson itself." He smiled, handing me his pen and paper. *Hold on* I thought this was supposed to be my lesson?

I took the pen anyway, puzzled. What was I supposed to do with it?

"Write, Ms Dakota. Listen and write."

I did as was instructed of me.

"What exactly am I writing, Doctor?" I stared at the paper, a blank page, confused and above all quite reluctant about agreeing to involve myself with any kind of scientific research. This kind of stuff was beyond. However, I empathised with Doctor Harvard's current position. He had agreed to learn about the things that interested me. It was only right that I complied with his wishes.

"I would like you to research and define the term 'Gradient'. Read up on it and perhaps try and solve some problems yourself? They shouldn't be too hard, but it is most likely that you will struggle to grasp the concept at first." He smirked at this point. This was an intentional dig at me. One of which he was aware I would retaliate to.

"Doctor Harvard, correct me if I am wrong, but I am quite certain that gradient is associated with mathematics?" I stared, simultaneously puzzled and relieved.

He smiled again, adjusting his glasses and rubbing his forehead.

"Correct, Ms Dakota. Now, you just have to define it and use it." He clapped sarcastically, to which I rolled my eyes. I had become immune to his humour now.

"I shall try my best... sir?" I winced.

"Doctor, Ms Dakota. I didn't earn this title for it not to be used." He rose, brushing himself off.

"Doctor, we still have ten minutes of the lesson left!?" I shouted, annoyed and bothered.

"Ms Dakota! My goodness, you are somewhat more attractive when angry. "He laughed to himself, closing the door gently but before shutting it completely, leaned his head round the frame of the door.

"Don't forget the research… Carrie." He smirked jokingly. I sat, puzzled about what had just happened. Doctor Harvard was at times so indecipherable that it frustrated me. This frustration overrode my curiosity to decipher his enigmatic personality, so much so, that I stopped thinking about it. Gradient? Why Gradient? I thought for a while but no possible conclusion entered my mind.

I sat on my chair, logged onto the school computers with my personal ID. I opened up safari and typed into Google advanced search 'The exact definition of Gradient'. I was overwhelmed by several definitions that came up. One definition titled 'Physics' described gradient as 'A curve representing such a rate of change.' Another mathematical definition, claimed that gradient referred to 'the slope of the tangent at any point on a curve.' It then dawned on me. Had Doctor Harvard given me this definition to research on purpose? Was it supposed to be interpreted as a metaphor for the change in my life? Was it some kind of metaphor? Was I reading too much into it? Could it be that he was mocking me? I sincerely hoped he wasn't but even if that was in fact his intention, it was undeniably genius.

7

Doctor Harvard's Lesson One: Gradient

I woke up, still thinking about the significance of Gradient and about what it all meant. I had Doctor Harvard's lesson today and this was the thought that overrode the significance of all others. The anticipation was irritating.

Finally, it was time for Doctor Harvard's lesson. I collected my things that I had organised the night before after my research was completed. I would be lying if I said I wasn't scared about how this lesson would go. Nevertheless though, I was determined to find out what Doctor Harvard's intentions were in requesting that I research this one thing.

I endured that sickening walk down the mile of scientific and mathematical information that practically lunged itself at me. I felt like a child being forced to go on the Ghost Train at the fair, turning my head in opposite directions to try and see which laboratory was the right one. Doctor Harvard's was titled 'Lab G'. I sauntered around, trying to find it and then, in the corner of my eye, I noticed a long white lab coat and Doctor Harvard's face poke out from the side of the door. I blushed a deep red, as, not only did this man already despise my subject and think that I was of a lower level of intelligence to him, he would now and quite rightly, be provided with evidence clarifying the truth of these opinions. I mean honestly, an English teacher not being able to find a lab; pathetic.

"Carrie." Doctor Harvard grinned, adjusting his glasses involuntarily.

"James." I smiled, staring at my feet that were now inexplicable dancing by themselves.

"Please, come in, make yourself at home." Doctor Harvard extended his arm which pointed in the direction of the many tables in the room. *Make myself at home?!* Was this really the most appropriate sentence to use?

I sauntered in reluctantly, refusing to look at any of the scientific imagery scattered proudly around the classroom. Doctor Harvard stared amusingly at me like I was an artefact he had once upon a time wanted to write many critical reviews on.

"Out of your element, Carrie? If you'll pardon the pun." He laughed briefly, adjusting his glasses again.

"Doctor Harvard. Why did you assign me Gradient to research?" I spoke sternly, not at any moment taking my eyes away from his.

He broke eye contact immediately. Moving over to his whiteboard and totally ignoring my question, proceeded on with his lesson.

"So, let's start with the …"

"DOCTOR HARVARD!" I shouted. I was frozen and immovable. The only signal identifiable that blood still pumping around my body was the tears, warm and multiplying that temporarily blurred my vision.

"Please, I am a human being, do not mock me. Answer my question." I remained still and tense. Doctor Harvard stood, still with his back to me and staring down at his hands. Slowly, he turned. The 5 seconds that felt like hours were over.

A Doorstep Miracle

"My intention was never to mock you, Ms Dakota, it was supposed to provide me with an insight into your mind."

"Oh! So now I'm a psychological experiment?! Brilliant." I got up and went to tuck my chair in when Doctor Harvard sprinted over to the other side of the room. He pushed my chair back in with force. I was shocked and above all, angry. I could feel perspiration on my forehead and my body temperature increased drastically.

"What on earth are you doing?! I screamed, placing my hand helplessly on the top of my head. I tried to run out of the classroom but was immediately restrained.

"Stop. Carrie. Stop." Doctor Harvard held me tight in his arms. I attempted several times to escape in a temper but failed. How was he capable of restraining me? His frame appeared incapable of holding me. After a few minutes, I gave up, my muscles relaxed and I fell, slumped into his arms, crying hysterically. Doctor James Harvard was the one who held me in that moment. In the moment when I could physically feel my entire world, cemented together again with weak materials and feigned emotions, crashing down carelessly.

"Let it go, Carrie." Doctor Harvard whispered in my ear whilst supporting my head up like I was a new born baby. After a while had passed, we sat in silence. Doctor Harvard stared at me whilst I wiped my face, laughing at what a fool I had been.

"James... I, I apologise. I've been foolish." My voice sounded broken and croaking, revealing surreptitiously, the gigantic lump in my throat that meant I was going to cry again.

He glared, with an almost angry look I his eyes.

"Foolish…hmm. What for? Expressing your feelings? Being yourself? Breaking down after being brave for too long?" Doctor Harvard's face remained still and the only thing that moved was his mouth. It was like he was now fed up. Fed up and exhausted with pretending.

"I hated my life, I hated the world and I hated myself. I blamed myself for the death of my parents and I took it out on everyone, everything, including myself. I took it out on writing. That was until I had the pleasure of meeting you and when I did, all of that changed. I had something to live for, someone to talk to. Do not apologise to me. Do not even dare apologising again in my laboratory because I will not allow it." I'll be darned, but to this day I recall Doctor James Harvard having tears in his eyes when speaking about me. It was emotion in its purest form. It was everything that constitutes us as human and I for one could not bring myself to take my eyes away from the sight. I sat, wide-eyed with my mouth open. No one since John had ever even noticed me or had ever shown this level of emotion towards me. I was starting to believe that no one ever would. I smiled with tears rolling down my cheeks.

"Can we continue with the lesson… please?" I smiled, tying my hair up in an attempt to salvage whatever normality was left amongst the shattered pieces of me, scattered on the floor that I had left.

Doctor Harvard smiled, this time taking off his glasses. He came and sat next to me.

"I admire your resilience, Carrie." Doctor Harvard grabbed my hand, squeezing it reassuringly.

"Thank you, James." I squeezed his hand back, staring at my paper, ready to learn.

A Doorstep Miracle

"Carrie, I assigned you Gradient as the subject because I knew that you would interpret it the way you did. I aimed for the reaction you gave because I want you to release your anger and let these emotions go. I consider myself a friend now, Carrie. The last time I checked, a friend was someone who you can rely on and talk to if you have any problems."

"I understand. Telling the truth, I was impressed by your metaphor. Gradient? The change in rate? Rate being my life and the change being John's death? That's seriously poetic and abstract. It was unorthodox, unexpected and genius. Thank-you. You're right, we are friends now and you should be proud of your progression. I hope one day, you'll pluck up the courage to write again. Who knows, you might even enjoy it?" I asked, shrugging.

"I sincerely hope that too, Carrie. I sincerely do." He smiled, grabbing his glasses and relocating them back to their rightful position on his face.

We spoke about gradient and as we were speaking, I was taking notes on it. It began to feel like a one on one revision session for an exam that I had forgotten to revise for and now I only had several hours to write up on it. I hated writing in short hand because I was afraid I would misinterpret some of my notes which would throw me entirely off track. I had to remember everything he had told me. I scribbled away and before we knew it the lesson was over. Something he said about gradient was sticking in my mind like a tongue stuck to ice; immovable. He told me that 'the higher the gradient, the steeper the line.' Lord knew he was right about that. Well, that was if he meant it in a metaphorical sense because, you know how us English fanatics like to interpret things that aren't there. But I questioned the possibility of his intention. What if he meant it like that? It was either that or a beautiful accident.

A Doorstep Miracle

"Thanks, James. I'll see you tomorrow, yes?" I carried my notes with me, holding them close like they were the most sacred object in the universe.

"You will, Carrie." He smiled, waving goodbye. I reciprocated and shut the door. Walking away, the posters on the walls no longer stared gloomily over me. The hallway appeared brighter than before and the titles on the labs, clearer. I walked on and as I did, I had that urge that only writers will understand. That fuse that is lit when you have an idea for a story. The adrenaline was racing through me. I was inspired and I had to write as soon as possible. I made some notes on the paper that I had, jotting potential dialogue, characters, locations, events, you name it, I was doing it and not a thing on this earth could stop me. Not while I was in this zone.

But as I was walking, oblivious to the rest of civilisation, I heard the most thought provoking, mindboggling question. I looked over my shoulder only to find a group of students towering over a young boy with Auden's 'Funeral Blues' in his hands. He was reading it to himself, practising I presumed. I didn't want to ask. But the question asked to the boy by the other students confirmed the truth of this assumption.

"Do you really think that reading that is going to bring your grandfather back to life? Are you going to go write about how shit life is you little emo? " One child said in a sharp, sarcastic tone followed by an assembled laughter from the other kids that pierced through my ears, so much so that I could feel the young boy's pain. I looked at the little boy. I stared at him. He could not see me but I could certainly see him. I could see his pain and I could feel his pain and the intensity of it was indescribable. Beads of tears formed on the lower part of his eye socket and they began to fall, relentlessly like the inevitability of a tide smothering the sea shore. I had felt it too, the pain he felt.

A Doorstep Miracle

But I could not stand back and persist in being an innocent bystander to this inexcusable act of viciousness. I once read that place in hell are reserved for those who maintain their neutrality in moments of moral crisis. I was not going to take my seat.

A wave of heat surged through me. At once I had forgotten what my position was in the school. I even forgot I was in a school. I forgot about everything for those moments and as soon as my mouth opened it was too late for me to stop. I stood. I towered. I stared. Deeper. Deeper and deeper still until the boy who had executed that disgusting sentence was paralysed. I bent down to the side of his head and whispered in his ear.

"Listen here you little shit, I'm not going to ask you to apologise to him because I know you don't mean it but I'll tell you something, he can write about it all he damn well likes and he could sure as hell write a book on how much of an asshole you are, get the picture? If you don't move right this second, I'll have him read a few draft extracts to the entire assembly hall. Is the picture perfect yet?" I leant up, staring at him still with anger in my eyes. I felt it so intensely that I was sure something had possessed me, taken over my body because it just wasn't like me. But I had never felt so satisfied for saying it, even if the realisation that I could lose my job began to kick in.

He stared, wide-eyed and open mouthed in shock. Slowly, he began to pace backwards. His pace then increased when he began to almost sprint out into the courtyard. I looked down at the little boy who was staring at me also in shock. I placed my hand gently on his shoulder.

"He won't be bothering you again...erm." I paused, waiting for him to announce his name.

"Tobias." He whispered breathlessly like he had laid eyes on a ghost.

"Tobias. He won't be bothering you anymore, okay?" I smiled reassuringly.

"Okay." He said, still wide eyed in shock.

"You just keep writing, okay? Never stop. I am sorry for your loss, Tobias." I squeezed his shoulder, staring at the poem he held, still with pride even though the other kids tried to knock him down and strip him naked of passion. He reminded me of myself. In fact… he reminded me of a young Doctor James Harvard. A young boy who had his passion stolen by the world, a world that stomped on it, screwed it up and threw it out like a disposable plastic cup. I walked away silently as I could feel tears slowly forming. My throat swelled and I couldn't swallow.

That night, I went home and I thought about my younger self. I thought about the amount of futile attempts people would take in order to knock me down. I wondered, how on earth did I overcome it? It all seemed almost apocalyptic to me at that age. I thought that being different was a curse some higher power bestowed on me but as I got older, I realised that difference is what people crave. They enjoy, revel in the idea of overthrowing order, subversion, exceeding boundaries. Was it possible, that I could help James exceed his? And in exceeding his, was I really just exceeding mine?

8

Ms Dakota's Lesson Two: creative writing

Today was another lesson. It was another chance for Doctor Harvard to prove to himself that he could do this. I was going to provide him with the strength, making him feel capable of doing this for himself. After all, he was a good writer, he had potential. It seemed criminal to supress such a talent.

I waited for him with a steaming cup of Coffee, several books that I had chosen accompanied by the piercing sound of afternoon rain slapping violently against the window. I had *'All shook up'* by Elvis Presley playing on my classroom stereo to lighten the mood. I sincerely hoped that James didn't interpret this in the wrong way. Perhaps he would think that this was an attempt to seduce him... oh God, hopefully not.

I waited for some time until I heard a knock at the door against the classroom door. It startled me slightly, causing me to jump out of my seat and drop my pencils everywhere.

"James! Come in, please." I spoke with a smile in my voice.

He opened the door, closing it carefully and with a darting glare I could sense his fear radiating across the room as his eyes were fixed on the stack of books that I had lying on my desk. He swallowed quickly and with force, adjusted his glasses. It was then established that he was nervous.

"Literature... books...?" James's entire being trembled as though a sharp cold breeze had passed him and tapped him on the back. The raising of his eyebrows had also signalled irritation.

"Oh… James, honestly it is a vital part of the lesson I assure you. It's for your benefit." I smiled, collecting the books together rather clumsily. As I did, I turned the volume on the stereo down.

"Is it? Or is it for your benefit?" James stared me up and down and then looked out of the window with a blatant expression of anger smothered across his face.
I stared, gobsmacked.

"And what in hell are you implying by that?!" I raised my voice, dropping the books immediately onto the floor and kicking them underneath one of the desks in the classroom. I stared up back at James, flustered and annoyed.

"Fine. Have it your way. We won't analyse any literature today! I was going to use them so that you could perhaps test out different writing styles to see which one you liked the best. Well, what do I know, huh? How stupid of me to believe that that would work." I sighed, leaning backwards on the surface of the desk with a carelessness expected from that of a rebellious, spiteful teen.

James remained silent, still obstinately staring out of the window to avoid eye contact and even conversation.

"What is it going to take? When will you leave your fear behind James? That part of your life is over and you are still allowing it to dictate your direction. I just want you to write but I guess, you don't want to write. And maybe you're right!? I can't make you. Maybe I am trying to fix myself by fixing you? I don't know but all I know is, is that I see a potential in you that shouldn't be supressed." I spoke, staring at my feet the whole time. Suddenly, I heard the rustling of pages and the scraping of a chair being pulled underneath a desk. My God. My mind prohibits me from ever erasing the sight from my memory. Doctor James Harvard was sitting at a desk in my classroom reading Mary Shelley's *'Frankenstein'* with an insouciance that prompted a nervousness in me, causing me to giggle.

"We better get started then. Shall we?" James smiled, holding out his hand as if he were inviting me to dance. I was as confused as I ever could be and the funniest part was that I could have sworn that approximately 10 seconds ago, he was going to destroy my classroom in a Hulk-style manor. Well, if Doctor Harvard didn't epitomise surprise, I don't know what did.

I smiled eagerly, taking his hand and grabbing a chair. I sat beside him whilst he turned the pages of chapter one. We read through to chapter five and then stopped. James was mesmerised momentarily and I had noticed that he was swallowing frequently again like he was trying to remove something from his throat.

"James, are you alright?" I rubbed his back gently.

"Yes. Please, let's carry on, I'd rather not talk about it." He nudged my hand away from his back with his shoulder and resumed an enclosed, introverted posture.

I was no genius, no psychologist, certainly no scientist but I wholeheartedly believed that my diagnosis was one hundred percent accurate. Doctor James Harvard had connected with a book and he was scared. He was scared to the core because he had identified his feelings inside something that he had over time developed a contempt for. It seemed anomalous to him. His attempts to understand the science behind this, failed because the thing is, sometimes there does not have to be rules and regulations in life and sometimes there are no explanations for the things that happen to us, they simply just happen. But he could never accept that. He had become immune to his logical way of thinking that there was no room for alternative interpretation.

"Would you rather write it down?" I urged, pushing a piece of blank, lined paper in front of him with a pen.

He stared at me and then down at the pen repeatedly with contemplation.

"How many minutes do I have to write?" He asked, adjusting his glasses.

"I'd expect you to be done within around five minutes. We'll see how you do, yes?" I smiled encouragingly, nodding my head briefly in the direction of the pen.

"Five minutes. Okay." He smiled, picking up the pen enthusiastically and starting to write. It was like he was unfamiliar with what paper was. It was like he was unfamiliar with what a pen was but one thing of which he was familiar was that these feelings were real. These feeling were truth and more specifically, he was familiar with the fact that they had been locked away for an eternity and had far exceeded their expiry date.

It was ten seconds until five minutes was up and the nervous tapping of James's pen only contributed to the intensity of the moment.

Five minutes was up and it was time to hear the verdict.
I bit my lip, simultaneously excited and anxious.

Our eyes locked immediately. He then stacked the pieces of paper up strategically, preparing to read them.

"Read." I said, on edge and remaining stood up for the occasion.

Doctor Harvard stared in disbelief at his paper but nevertheless, wet his lips and began to read. At first, he struggled with an irritating stutter to say even the first word.

"It's alright James. It's just me, remember? Carrie." I smiled reassuringly whilst tugging at my clothes to remind him that I was nothing and no one special and that I certainly wasn't anybody he needed to impress.

Finally, he plucked up the courage, opened his mouth and began to read. And when he did, well, I swear from that day forward, I believed in miracles.

"Like a covalent bond, I have remained unbreakable, statuesque and superior. Like an iceberg, I appear inferior and weak on the surface but with the equivalent to the world's mass, lie beneath the ocean of people that I do endure, my pains, flaws and futile attempts to enjoy the life that was once bestowed. Like death, I will acquire your last breath and frame it on my wall and in my trophy cabinet alongside former victims and with the click of a fingers I will rearrange your life until finding your soul again is like playing a game of Guess Who... I-"

"Enough. Enough." I interrupted with a lump that swelled increasingly in my throat. I stared at the ground, breathing deeply with tears rolling down my cheeks.

"Carrie." James spoke in a concerned tone to which I held my hand out in front of my face.

"Please. I am fine." I insisted, wiping my face with the back of my hand in embarrassment. I looked up at James without a word and I simply stared for a few seconds.

"That… that was beautiful." I could hardly speak. It was as though I were miming the words.

James stared at his paper, incredulous. He couldn't actually believe that he had written it himself and then the realisation hit him, the epiphany that he could write. The realisation that every writer has felt before. It was that feeling when you know that what you have written has touched someone and to know that someone out there in this world has felt what it is that you are feeling. Quite ironically, there are no words to describe it.

"Thank you, Carrie, are you alright? You look as though you're going to…" He hesitated, struggling to finish his sentence when he realised the inappropriate choice of vocabulary considering the current situation.

"Die? Ha-ha." I laughed with my head thrown back. "Oh, James that is impossible. I am already dead." I continued to cry silently and without expression.

James walked over to me but I refused to be smothered with sympathy. I was stronger than that and I could fight this. It was just the shock of the moment. It was so overwhelmingly beautiful that I couldn't help but cry because it touched me, it really touched me and from that moment I knew that James was going to be a writer. A brilliant, admirable, bestselling writer and I couldn't have thought of anyone more deserving of receiving the honour. It is rarely that I read a piece that inspires me and this principle I assumed applied to that of a piece which is verbally expressed. However, there is a first time for everything and for the first time in what felt like an eternity, I was wholeheartedly inspired. I couldn't stop crying. I had once read that language opens doors. Doors were beginning to open for me. More importantly though, doors into rooms beyond the standard imagination were being opened for James and it thrilled me to watch him progress. Knowing that he truly deserved this, I felt like I was fighting for something again. I felt that perhaps there were reasons for getting up in the morning. Doctor James Harvard, the symbol of hope, hope when hope seems a distant memory.

"So, I trust you have set me additional work for outside of lessons?" James smirked.

"Indeed I have, Doctor Harvard." I reciprocated with a corresponding smirk.

"What is the task? Or do I dare not ask?" James winced with clenched teeth.

"Oh don't be so ridiculous! I wouldn't set you anything unless I knew you could handle it and I know for a fact, especially after that, that you can indeed." I smiled, purposely widening my eyes to emphasise my judgement.

"I have to ask, Carrie. Were you telling the truth when you said my piece was beautiful?" James stared patiently, half expecting me to say that I what I said was a lie and that the only reason I said it was to make him feel better about himself.

"James. Honestly, I could have told you that your piece was adequate, satisfactory, standard, but you see, I've never really been one for telling lies and those of which I've told can only be the ones that I have told myself. I would be lying if I told you that your piece was terrible because I swear to you in this room in this moment, you shocked me. But truthfully, I always knew you had it in you. Has anyone ever told you James that you're much like a volcano? Your imagination has been dormant for so long and only now has it chosen to erupt. Funny thing isn't it?" I smiled, touching his hand and squeezing it reassuringly.

"Well then, I have only you to thank for providing me with the courage to believe that I could do it." James stared, squeezing my hand tighter. There was a mutual understanding that we were both extremely grateful for having met each other and for having made these arrangements.

There we sat.

Silence.

Four hands and the ticking of a clock.

"Doctor Harvard, I think you are ready for a prescription." I smiled, handing him my copy of Shelley's *Frankenstein*.

"I can't accept this. It's awfully kind of you but you see, I feel terrible taking this." James's hand hovered over the book in contemplation to accept the offer.

"You're not taking it. I am giving it to you as a gift. Receive your gift. I trust you're familiar with the concept of a gift are you not?" I giggled, smiling at him and wrapping his fingers around the spine of the book as though I were handing over someone's baby to them.

James did not say a word, accepting the book, he held it tightly like some sacred object. I believe he worshipped it, like how a Christian worships the Bible. He appeared like a student starting a new school, eager to learn with brand new equipment.

"And what does one call the pharmacy from which I am able to collect more supplies, should I require a higher dosage?" James grinned, playing along.

"I believe good sir, you shall find that the only pharmacy distributing this type of medicine is called the Library." I grinned, laughing as I did.

I hugged James and he thanked me for the lesson. I told him that he was more than welcome and that if he had any questions that he could call me on my mobile or even turn up at my house. I could feel our friendship developing and I enjoyed every moment of it. It was refreshing, knowing that you had a friend, someone to trust and someone who trusted you. No judgement for my imperfections and flaws. Just two people who openly accepted imperfection as it should be accepted.

He walked out, closing my door and I was back to square one again. Me, myself and my oh-so-clingy emotions. They were like a leech against my heart that had no blood to give, yet, the possibility for blood to be drained of my being was far from an impossibility but rather now, a reality. I think I needed James. I think I needed James because he was a reflection of myself and I needed to know that it could be possible for other people to be able to feel the same way as I did just so that I wasn't alone in my isolation.

9

The beginning of the end

As the days passed along with the increase in lessons that James and I had together, I began to identify a thing in him that was the closest thing to magic I had ever known. His writing style developed along with his ideas. I was starting to think that maybe he didn't get his degree in science but in English language. He was asking frequently to borrow books from my shelf and these consisted for teaching purposes, of the literary classics like *Great Expectations*, *Dracula, Sense and Sensibility* and *Wuthering Heights.*

I would sometimes just stare at him reading and I would wonder what went on in his mind and about how hard he was working. He would start to hide a selection of paper notes in the pages of books which initially I perceived to be book marks. But again, just like he had surprised me before, James had been writing. His notes weren't just notes, but extracts for a project which he had been working on, I later discovered.

"James…let me see those notes? They look pretty thought-provoking…what's on them?" I enquired, cocking my head sideways in extreme interest.

He speedily covered his notes by clamping them down with one of the books that I had let him borrow.

"Err. Err, I will show you soon but not now, do you mind?" He said quietly whilst adjusting his glasses.

I laughed outrageously and skipped towards him. Jokily I tried to snatch the notes to which James persisted in hiding. Finally, I succeeded in grabbing one of the notes and started reading some of them out.

"STOP. Please, don't Carrie." He pleaded. But I wasn't listening. I was oblivious to it because I was wrapped up in a whole separate mentality. I taunted him like a childish bully, grabbing his notes and waving them viciously in front of his face knowing full well that he couldn't catch them.

"Oooooo, James, well I say... what have we here! Hahaha!" I laughed which sounded more like a shriek than a laugh. I then looked down at the words that were written in front of me and my heart collapsed with guilt. I was existentially entrapped for that single moment and would have given anything to not have read those notes. That's the thing though, isn't it? You cannot, no matter how hard you try, erase the past. I analysed closely, turning over the notes and then it was confirmed. Extracts of dialogue? Names of characters and fictional settings... Doctor James Harvard was writing a novel?

I gasped. I stared up at him and I gasped.

"James. James, you're...you're writing a novel?" I stared, my eyebrows raised and lips pursed.

"You're angry." He said with monotony.

"NO! I...I'm not angry." I rubbed my face with my hand, burying my face followed by yet again, another sigh.

James stared down at the floor and then up at me repeatedly.

"You didn't think to tell me? Why wouldn't you tell me about this?" I stood, shaking my head in disappointment.

"I. I didn't want you to think that I was stealing your spotlight. I mean, you're a writer and I'm a science teacher. It's not orthodox to expect a science teacher to write a novel." James spoke, apologetically and adjusted his glasses.

"James, everybody is a writer…some just haven't realised it yet." I spoke, softly.

James looked up, blinking frantically.

"And don't you see James? That's the beauty of this. It's not expected of you and yet you are pursuing it? Exceeding expectations. That is the beauty of life. It can tear you down but at the same time it can show you yourself in ways you never comprehended possible." I leant down to James at eye level and slapped my hands hard on the desk. I stared at him the entire time and not once did I blink.

"You can't steel a spotlight where there is no electricity with which it can be lit." I smiled. "I haven't written in 6 months because the thing that inspired me died and it took my soul with it."

"Excuse me, I may be getting a bit personal here, but does that not give you more of a reason to write?" James stared, waiting for the answer like his life depended on it. I avoided the question.

"I, I just thought you'd react differently. I thought you'd be angry." James fiddled with his hands and gave an apologetic stare.

"Angry, yes of course I'm fucking angry. You didn't tell me you were writing a novel when I have been the one to teach you all this time. I want to share your success with you, not tear it down." I gave a disappointing look and turned around to face the window. Perhaps the natural view of trees, sunshine and birds with no worries that soared would distract me from the complicated emotions of the human mind which remain an unanswered question in civilisation. Sure, Darwin provided us with an explanation of evolution but he left out the parts about the evolution of the human heart.

"I'm sorry. I should have told you. Perhaps I should leave." James shifted his chair and appeared ready to leave.

"Oh no you don't. You're not going anywhere until you explain these notes." I grabbed his arm tightly and tugged him until he sat back down in his seat.
James stared blankly at me in confusion. To which I stared back incredulously.

"Well, you have to get these published?" I held the notes in front of my face and proceeded to read.

"My heart ached with an anguish incurable by the means of orally inserting any pharmaceutical medicine advised by any qualified doctor. Have you ever felt stuck, in love, in life? I know you have. I know you have because I have and you are my reflection. The fire in your eyes scorches my soul and it is not oxygen which does fuel its power but instead, your touch against my skin which feels like the beginning stages of an explosion." I stopped reading. Put the note down and I sighed deeply.

"Do you know how frustrating it is when someone with potential doesn't believe in themselves? When someone doesn't know how good they really are?" I buried my head in my hands despairingly.

"Thank you Carrie. I mean it. Thank you but I simply can't publish anything. It would be totally out of the blue and so… well, I'm not like you, I wouldn't have the courage to continue." James bowed his head in disbelief and it made me die inside.

"What are you so scared of? Why are you so scared? So what if it's out of the blue it's fucking good!" I held in intense stare.

"I'm not publishing anything! Damn it Carrie! I can't." James's head sloped downwards and his entire face dropped.

"You're scared about selling your feelings, aren't you? Because this isn't just notes and a story but this is actually about you." I leant forward to touch James's hand but he flinched.

"Well, aren't you smart?" he replied sarcastically. There was a moment of silence.

"Hey, don't do that to me. Don't treat me like a fucking child, we've shared too much for you to be talking to me like that. You know and I know I'm right. And it doesn't make me clever, it makes me truthful. You should try it some time." I got up and paced up and down the room like James had done in his laboratory when we first met.

"Truth? What would you know about truth? You're an English Teacher. You know fiction and you know disguise. What better way to disguise the truth than with words, hmm?" There was an immediate look of regret smothered across James's face just as the words he had spoken left his mouth.

I darted a long and hard stare at James. It was so intimidating that I was even scared of myself for a moment. I was scared for the other person inside me to be released. I didn't want to be that person. I had been so many people but I couldn't do it anymore. I wanted so badly to be someone else.

"Truth? You want to know about truth, huh? Sure, we can talk about truth if you'd like, because I know I would. I really really would Doctor James Harvard." I stepped slowly towards James's desk and I stood, towering over him.

"Truth is realising that when your mother and father are shouting so loud at each other that you can barely think it is probably time for you to move along and live your life somewhere else. Truth is when you are incapable of hurting because for so long, you have been missing that person who made you feel complete. Truth is a beaten mother with two black eyes that are so sewn together with blood she can hardly see. So, I apologise if my definition of the truth differs from yours, James, but don't you dare, ever, insinuate that I am unfamiliar with the term. I may be hurt, damaged but I am not stupid." I pointed my finger in James's face until my hand shook so much with anger, you would have thought I had Parkinson's.

There was a long silence. We did not speak. We did not share eye contact.

"I'm sorry Carrie. I shouldn't have said that, I should have known it was going to set you off." James walked and stood beside me putting his hand comfortingly on my shoulder. I cared for James. I really cared for James but sometimes I questioned it. Then I started to realise that this is how parents must feel about their children. Unconditional love; it wasn't what Doctor James Harvard called a 'covalent bond' but it was sure as hell the strongest bond I think I've ever known.

I turned to face James and I placed my hand on his left shoulder.

"I know you are and I apologise too." I smiled, adjusting his glasses. They had fallen from their usual position on his face. "Thanks, James." I said, smiling meaningfully.

"What for are you thanking me?" He replied, oblivious to how he had been responsible for making my life make sense to me again.

"For being you and for never stopping. You inspire me, Doctor James Harvard. You inspire me to be the best that I can be and if possible better than I can be. You are a great writer, never stop." I whispered in his ear. He grinned back laughing and adjusting his glasses.

"Is that really what you want?" James said, rubbing my shoulder.

"With every ounce of my being." I smiled.

"Then it shall be done, but remember I am doing this for you because it was because of you that I am doing this." He smiled smugly.

"You're publishing your work?!" I grabbed James's shoulder eagerly and squealed like an excited child.

James smiled, staring at his feet and then back at me.

"I am publishing my work." He grinned with gleaming eyes and for once in all the time that I had known him, there was colour that had been restored again like some miracle, some unnoticed, unrecognised miracle, a doorstep miracle.

"Well, we have to get the publishers on the phone right away! I mean, we have to make things official. James, are you hungry? Do you want a drink? Wait, of course you do, hold on I'll get you at Tea. Do—"

"Carrie! Please!" James grinned, giggling and pulling out a chair for me to sit on. "Calm down, please. First thing's first, I want to say a few words."

Words? What on earth could James possibly have to say to me? Was he even excited? Was he doing this just for me? Did he want this? Any of this?

"I don't understand... it only takes a few seconds, I don't mind James!" I smiled with excitement in my voice.

"No, it's not that Carrie. I just want to talk to you, about us." He smiled, adjusting his glasses and tapping the back of the chair for me to sit on it.

About us? What could there possibly be?
I didn't say a word although I wished I had questioned him.

I sat.

I didn't speak.

"Carrie. I want you to take the royalties for the book." James spoke, adjusting his glasses so frequently, I thought they were going to fall off completely.

I sat with my mouth wide open.

"James, what... what on earth are you talking about?" I replied, raising my voice and widening my eyes whilst shaking my head in disapproval.

"I said, I want you to take the money from the book, should it earn anything."

"Oh James, there's no question of a doubt this stuff you've written will sell, I'm telling you, but taking your money, I mean no James!" I shook my head in disbelief at the proposal. "James, it's not even about the money or even about taking credit for the words in that book. I would be taking your heart, a part of your life."

"You wouldn't be taking it, you've been a part of it the whole time. It's basically a part of your life too." He wet his lips, adjusted his glassed and stared up at me with his smile that promised security. At times, I was frightened at the thought that I would never meet a person more kind than James for the rest of my life. I shivered at the thought that I could be so wrong about a person. James Harvard was a subversion, there wasn't anything on this earth that could disprove that fact and if you didn't see it, well, congratulations for your ignorance.

I struggled to speak and my lips quivered as I tried to conjure up a decent reply. But he was right. This part of his life, we had shared together but there was no way I was taking his money and I told him that. Finally, he got the picture and we refused to talk about it again. I called some publishers and sent them some extracts that I thought were the ones highlighting James's talent the most. Although, even this was a struggle, they were all so good, it was hard to choose.

Two hours later I received a call from a private publisher situated in Chicago.

"Hello, this is Janet Crenshaw calling, I represent Dream Catchers publishing house. We have just received your piece and we understand that you'd be interested in publishing? Would it be at all possible to speak with the author of this piece?" A woman called, she sounded cool, calm and collected.

"Hi, yes, I'll just hand you over. Excuse me one second." I placed my phone over the speaker and grinned excitedly. James stared in confusion and asked me who it was. I ignored his question and instead, handed the phone over to him.

"He...Hello?" James answered the phone, nervous and with his voice shaking.

"Hello, Mr Harvard?" The woman asked, with such as high-pitched voice that I could hear her from where I was standing.

"Doctor. And yes, this is him, can I help?" James was adjusting his glasses again and fiddling with his jumper sleeves.

"Well, the question is Doctor, can we help!? We have just received your piece here at Dream Catchers publishing house and would love to make you an offer!" She was extremely convincing. She sounded too happy to be human, I'm sure she was a robot, I'm sure of it.

Oh, I see. Well, what offer were you going to make?"

"If your book sells, we will be taking twenty percent royalties, meaning that you would be earning eighty percent, all in all, you would be earning more, of course. I'd just like to point out, Doctor Harvard, that we do not do this usually. We usually only offer a forty percent sixty percent offer and sometimes even fifty fifty. You are genuinely our only exception."

James looked at me in a way that I will never forget. He was scared and confused like a naive child. It was like he had been given this responsibility with no idea about how to manage it. I think for once in his life he found himself without knowledge.

I scurried over to the phone and took it off of James who didn't fight it. I think he was shocked, shocked that something he had written had even been noticed.

"Hello, this is James's friend, he is elated and would love to accept the offer. Thank you." I have never spoken so quickly in my life.

"Excellent. Of course for legal reasons we would have to have a hard copy of Doctor Harvard's signature on the form for identification and consent. We will keep in touch and thanks again for choosing our publishing house, good day!" The girl hung up the phone almost immediately.

"James, congratulations!" I ran and hugged him. He hugged me back and smiled, although I could tell that he felt strange. "You're happy, right?"

"Happy, why, of course but it's just, I don't deserve this." He stared in guilt over at my books and around my classroom that appeared as though a thousand words off of a book had exploded onto the walls.

"James, can I be honest with you?" I grabbed his jumper tightly and stared up at him.

"I don't know what it is we've been doing for the past few months but, of course." He laughed.

"Don't ever think that you're not deserving of this because of me or for that matter because of anyone. People enjoy seeing others hurt, it makes them feel safe. But guess what? I'm not one of those people James, I care about you a lot and I believe in you. I believe in writing and I believe you can do this. This is just the beginning, the beginning of the end." I stared up and kissed James on the cheek. I noticed his face change completely from laughter to solemnity in 2 seconds flat. His eyes began to fill up with tears and then they fell, without restrain, without permission, they fell.

"Thank you." James whispered in my ears, hugging me again.

"No, thank you." I whispered back.

10

'I do believe in miracles, I do, I do.'

A week had passed since James received the form from Dream Catcher's publishing house and the truth had presented itself in the form of 600 copies of James's book demanded by readers across the country which he later titled '*Love: A separate science*'. The book was absolutely mind-blowing. He had received letters from online readers, some requesting book signings and even live readings. James had grown busy with these requests and although we still attended my lessons, it was more like an opportunity to catch up than to actually teach him anything. But somehow I knew he didn't really need it. I looked at him and I'd never felt so proud. I was the happiest I'd been in a long time and I still am.

James informed me that due to the amount of copies he had sold, he was due to have a book signing in the following week. He seemed nervous about this but I told him what I had always told him; be yourself, never stop, stay true to yourself, that's all you can do. I hope he listened. It so happened that I accidently bought an entry ticket to the book signing without James knowing. I didn't bother informing him, I wanted it to be a surprise. I told James that I couldn't attend and made an excuse about how many books I have to mark for my students, he believed me of course but it was hard to keep it a secret whenever I saw him. The signing was at 1:00am and I was going to be late if I didn't down this coffee that I had been staring at for the past three minutes. It was now 12:45 and the signing was ten minutes away.

I downed my coffee and spilt it all over my blouse. It was so typical of me to mess this up. I was always late. I

83

A Doorstep Miracle

jumped in my car and drove off speedily. I drove and as I
did I turned on the radio to the song *'All shook up'* by
Elvis Presley. This made me smile and I thought about all
the fun I'd had with James, how important it was that I met
him. One person can really change absolutely everything
and I was just starting to realise the importance. I stared at
the sun in my eyes and I imagined it to be John staring
down at me. I wanted him to be proud of me and to hold
me how he used to. Life was hard without him and it
would continue being a struggle but I couldn't give up
now, I wouldn't give up now, not now I'd come this far.

I arrived finally and was relieved to know that I hadn't
missed the signing or the live reading. The venue was
filled with writers and professors, James's book was a big
deal. Enlarged posters had been darted around the room
that was white and spacious with minimal furniture, like
an expensive modernised apartment or an art gallery. The
time was exactly 12:55. I had enough time to get a copy
signed. I spied a queue and started to get anxious. Then, by
some chance, a girl in front asked if I wanted to go in front
of her, it's like she knew. I jumped at the chance and only
had to wait for four more people to get their books signed.
I could see James faintly and he seemed introverted as
usual. I felt I should be there with him to calm him down
but no. This was his moment, I was going to let him have
it even if I desperately wanted to be there with him.

The queue was down to one more girl and I was behind
her. James didn't look up and my heart was beating fast. I
placed my book down.

"Who am I writing this out to?" James spoke, with
monotony.

"Ms Dakota, or perhaps, C or Carrie." I grinned as James's
head slowly rose he looked so shocked but elated at the
same time. He stood, hugging me.

"You… but…you couldn't make it? I don't …" James could hardly speak, it's like his mouth was paralysed on its own.

"Well, I'm here now and you Doctor, are a success, so, hurry up, you have a live reading to attend." I smiled, grabbing my book and walked over to the rows of seats near the podium on which James would stand. I stared back at James and he stared back at me. There was a mutual excitement between us which I hadn't felt since John. Although I didn't love James in the same way, I loved him nonetheless. I wasn't an expert on love and I wasn't familiar with different types of love but I knew they existed. Perhaps once I had read James's book, I'd understand.

It was 1:05 and James had finished his book signing. He was the escorted over by two gentlemen who represented Dream Catchers Publishing House. As he strolled over with a copy of his book held close to his chest I started to tear up. I felt like a mother on the day of her son's graduation.

The applause James received was that expected from a King. It was as though royalty had arrived. James stood on the podium, adjusting his glasses and sipping from a glass of water carefully balanced on the desk beside him. There was a sharp, piercing sound as James accidently hit the microphone.

"I apologise." He said, shaking and appearing flustered and nervous.

He looked at me in the crowd and I mimed the word 'breathe' to him to which he gave a short sharp nod and stared back at the microphone. There were easily hundreds of people that had attended. If there were anymore, James would have had to hire out an Arena. He calmed down quickly and focused.

"Hello, all. Thank you for attending my … my book signing. But before I start, I'd like very much to take the liberty of dedicating not only this entire book, but the past few months of my life, to none other than the intelligent, patient and warmest soul this world has to offer, to Ms Carrie Dakota." James spoke, elegantly and without so much as a stutter. I froze, swallowing hard as I felt the tears in my eyes begin to overflow. They blurred my vision and I could not stop them from falling now. Thousands of eyes were on me and I felt myself blush. There was a huge round of applause and through the ocean of people the only person I saw was James. He nodded, casually smiling at me as though no one else, not even this crowd of people mattered.

"I never once thought in all my life that science and literature would mix. I thought it to be an impossible combination, however, when reading Shelley's *Frankenstein*, I discovered that anything is possible. Even to be loved, despite how damaged you may be and believe me, I have been damaged beyond repair… or so I thought. Writing this book has given me a meaning, a purpose. I enjoy science and I love nothing more than science but when embarking on a project such as this, I cannot help but love writing, reading and even discussing writing. I am truly a different person and I believe that change is possible, whatever your circumstances may be. I have lived other people's lives through writing and I intend to tell more stories, but first, perhaps the beginning, is the perfect place to start." James held up his book with pride, bowing to the audience who were applauding wildly. I have never been so proud.

He gave a reading from the first chapter of his book. It was beautiful.

"And what is love? If not pain, then what? If not one love, then how many? I have been saved by love, taken by love and rescued from insanity. I have been served my own broken heart for breakfast and despite the fact that the human blood clots, mine refuses. Mine has been drained and served as a drink to remedy the broken, my heart, blended and made into a smoothie for the enjoyment of those seeking more than pure emotion, those scared of truth, there are many types of love, a separate science I have discovered." James closed the book immediately so as to suggest that if he continued he may reveal too much publicly. This was because it was okay for people to read about his heart and about his mind in the confines of four walls, but to be publically analysed whilst hurting, well, it would be agonising for anyone. I applauded first and louder than any other person sitting there. It was impossible for anyone to be more proud of him than I was because I knew the real Doctor James Harvard. James Harvard, a bigger man than most men will ever be. A man who gives his heart out for the world to see in the form of words on a page. James Harvard was a miracle, but not just any miracle, he was a doorstep miracle. One that happens secretively and with the upmost grace, a harvested talent that for so long has been concealed by the oppressive could that is the remains subsequent to death. But in the absence of the love he had once felt, somehow writing it all down was what bought it all back and he'd never loved more than in that moment when his feelings were truly appreciated.

Once he had stepped down from the podium followed by a bombardment of questions from various professors, he turned towards me and I stood, waiting patiently like an eager fan, his biggest fan.

"So, what do I call this brilliant author?" I smiled, giving James a look of extreme surprise.

"Why, hello, my name is Doctor Harvard." He replied, with a smile in his eyes.

"Doctor Harvard, please, call me Carrie." I laughed mischievously, holding my hand out and instigating a handshake and pretending like we had never met.

"Please, Carrie, call me James." He accepted, shaking my hand enthusiastically. We laughed outrageously and started to walk towards the doors. The live reading had finished and everything had come to an end, except from the lingering spirit of course. One which illuminated every dark path we had crossed. Instead, I came to realise that the only way from here was up and that is the direction in which I intended to venture.

"So, James, what is it that you do?" I asked with solemnity in an attempt to disguise my act.

"Well, I teach at a school just across the road." James also replied with solemnity, knowing wholeheartedly what I was doing.

"Ah, yes, I am familiar with it." I replied, trying to stifle my laughter through a crooked smile.

"Yes, so what is it you're into Carrie?" James asked, deliberately flicking through his book and pretending to read the last page.

"Oh, well, I'd say I'm partial to a discussion about quantum physics, and yourself?" I smiled, diverting my eye contact from him to the walls around me.

"Oh, well, I'd say I'm partial to a book or two being an author and all, I mean, can you imagine a life without reading a single book? I mean, you would only be living your life!" James shook the book in front of my face with emphasis.

"Oh, well, I wouldn't know, would you do me the honour of perhaps teaching me?" I acted oblivious which only contributed to the absurdity of the conversation.

We both stopped, stared at each other and laughed hysterically.

Silence prevailed once again and speech was not required.

Nothing was required.

Two people whose damaged souls had been mended by each other's weaknesses, such a tragically beautiful synergy, one which I would never in my life forget.

Sometimes all it takes is for someone to tell you that you can recover what you once lost, or what you thought you were incapable of discovering. And so, I decided that this winter, I would be the person to light a flame never once before lit and to challenge possibility with everything I knew, taking into consideration all consequences. And if you asked me "would you do this all over again?" I would answer with confidence "Absolutely."

I had been witness to life's cruelty, I had been witness to life's kindness but most of all I had been witness to a Doorstep miracle.

A Doorstep Miracle

CPSIA information can be obtained at www.ICGtesting.com
Printed in the USA
LVOW06s1804260815

451611LV00001B/44/P